I0461454

THE HARBINGER

Elec Twisiti

Twisiti Press

ISBN : 979-8-9894349-0-9 (eBook edition)
ISBN : 979-8-9894349-1-6 (Paperback edition)

Library of Congress Control Number: 2023920651

Artwork & Cover design by: Elec Twisiti

Printed and bound in the United States of America

First Edition : November 2023

PREFACE TO ADULTS

In less than 100 years, hand calculators have gone from a novelty to a required school supply. Over the last 20 years, they have gone from a simple tool to a hand-held graphics computer and an application on a smartphone. With the commercial release of multiple Artificial Intelligence (AI) tools in 2023, it is not too farfetched to posit that students may stop learning Mathematics and relying on software to provide all of the answers.

Since the dawn of the industrial revolution, our world has changed enormously and the emergence of AI is likely to spawn a new age. At its worst, AI will become a crutch used by businesses to maximize profits by minimizing payrolls, and for individuals to take shortcuts in their learning process as they seek to optimize their productivity. A new era, better or worse, is upon us.

So where does that leave children of this generation and those to come? Are we, the adults, the educators, the experts, the concerned parents, doing enough in our capacity to equip the young with the right tools for their future success?

Mass education is a great tool when the desired outcome is to impart a basic set of knowledge to as many children as possible. However, beyond the realm of academia, this top-down approach has been rendered obsolete as even the lowest ranking employee is now empowered and almost required to regularly go above and beyond their assigned duties. So rather than teaching to children, should we not follow suit and instead, empower them to learn? To let children discover their own path, absorb the world the way they see fit, and self-motivate to pursue their interests and dreams? What if we stop lecturing at students and instead provide guidance, inspiration and help when needed?

Within Mass Education, "standards" are necessary benchmarks to gauge the efficacy of the teaching, but they cannot strictly dictate how any child learns. Because, contrary to "standards," kids' interests follow no standard. As long as there is no punishment or social stigma for students who achieve differently or in their own time, children NATURALLY rise up to the challenges presented and they are eager to do more. Anybody who watches kids as they learn and play understands that education isn't about perfect scores, and answers to questions that are purged from their brains before they exit the school grounds. True Learning manifests itself in the passions of each person, their desire to investigate and to come to understand the why behind what is being explored. And only with True Learning, not top-down lecturing, may we allow those who are different to thrive, and hopefully we can see more to become great scientists like Michael Faraday, Thomas Edison,

Albert Einstein or many of the "drop-outs" who have created products and services in Silicon Valley that have profoundly changed the world.

Elec Twisiti is a pseudonym for a group of individuals who wanted to do better for the children in our lives. Inspired by the way so many great persons have self-taught after finding the hidebound educational systems of their eras to be inadequate, we have helped children of all ages achieve beyond what they or their parents imagined. We have guided average kids to achieve almost perfect scores for TOEFL, SAT and/or ACT in only a third of the time "required" by paid consultants. We enabled a 2nd grade student to achieve high percentiles for the 5th grade standardized tests in Math and Reading. With a dash of inspiration, we see an 8-year-old enjoying and understanding high school level Math, Biology, and Physics.

We believe that with the right support and triggers, any child can thrive and learn much faster than dictated by our rigid curricula. Learners new to this method often require more support at the beginning because they are no longer being spoon fed the curriculum, but once they see their own improvement, their self-confidence grows and they become more passionate about learning. Rather than becoming a victim of this new AI era, they will learn to rise above it to become active contributors to the new and better world.

This book is the first in a series that is crafted towards inspiring children and imparting knowledge in a fun and accessible way. It is the result of a decade working in education combined with multiple decades of working in corporate environments. We have combined the best of formal and hands-on knowledge and tried to use simple language to explain some complicated concepts. We aim to show the readers real-world applications of Math and Science and how easy it is to move from Elementary level math up into Middle School and beyond. But keep the dictionary handy as we want to expand your vocabulary and show the fun of language.

This story highlights the characteristics of young learners: their desires, their dreams, and their natural inclination towards learning. We use some fantastical elements to make the stories attractive to children and teach them some new Math tricks along the way. We hope the adults in the life of the learner will enjoy and learn from this book as well.

As much as we try to make the book free of error, if you, dear readers, find any mistake in the concepts we presented or have any other comments on the stories, kindly email us at stemdation@gmail.com.

Last but not least, we need to THANK all the teachers, educators, and parents who have and continue to work hard, to help change the status quo, despite numerous unsurmountable challenges. If you ever feel discouraged, please take comfort that your efforts have inspired us to embark on the same journey. Someday, somehow, your hard work will pay off.

PREFACE TO
THE YOUNG

There are some strict rules to follow while reading this book:

- When you giggle, do not jiggle your belly button.

- Create your own Math and Science challenges to share with your families and friends.

- If the book inspires you to dream big, we would love to hear from you, with your parent's permission, and hope you will pass along the book to help inspire others.

But the MOST important rule of all: Start reading and have fun!

This page is booooring – so move on.

Elec Twisiti

CHAPTER ONE

THE BROUHAHA

M r. Troubar, the Math Teacher at the Dozzaff School, hurried into the 5th grade classroom. He skipped saying hello to the students as he slammed his things down on his desk, then grabbed a piece of chalk and wrote out a crazy long number on the blackboard. He had it in for one of his students today and was anxious to get started.

"Amby! Read this number to the class!" demanded Mr. Troubar.

3,829,648,353.827

Near the back of the room, Amby tried to shrink down in his desk to evade Mr. Troubar's gaze. All he could think of was 'I can't.' He had never been good at Math and never really cared to improve his situation because he didn't see how it would help him achieve his dream of becoming a soccer superstar, like Messi or Ronaldo. But he didn't dream of fame or glory on the pitch, he dreamt about being able to help his family, and himself, crawl out of crushing poverty.

He hated living hand to mouth. He hated being the only kid who had to get free lunches at school and subsisting on the meager left-overs that his parents brought home from the restaurants they worked at. Every night, he wished he could dig into a big plate of fresh, steaming, and mouthwatering food. Was there anything wrong with that dream?!

Last Wednesday, he had spent two extra hours after soccer practice working on his own, leaving him no energy to finish his Math assignment that night. When he pulled out the worksheet the next morning, he was surprised to see that it had been fully completed. He felt weird because nobody in his family ever touched his work. He tried to ask his Mom about it, but she shooed him out the door so he would not be late for school.

As he sat in class, eyes locked with Mr. Troubar, Amby couldn't help but think that his impossibly perfect score on that assignment was the reason he was the center of attention today.

Mr. Troubar could see the fear in Amby's eyes, so he made a circle with his lips and stuck out his tongue, forming his mouth into a megaphone, and announced "Please go ahead, Amby!" so loudly it left all the kids' ears ringing like after a fire drill.

Amby's heart sank to his toes. He closed his eyes, desperate to arrange his thoughts. Tears quietly flowed down his cheeks. He took a deep breath to steady himself as he decided to tell Mr. Troubar that he had no idea. Like some horrible train wreck caught in slow motion, Amby slowly raised his head, opened his eyes, and was on the verge of apologizing when life resumed normal speed and without hesitation, the answer burst forth:

"Sir...Three billion, eight hundred twenty-nine million, six hundred forty-eight thousand, three hundred fifty-three and eight hundred twenty-seven thousandth.

Amby knew what he had just said, but he wasn't sure where the words had come from. And then, right before his eyes, like a transparent computer screen floating in front of him, he clearly saw a graphic of what he had uttered. He hit his forehead, then shook his head, but it was still there. He rubbed his eyes hard enough to bring fresh tears; it was still there. What the heck was going on? Where had this come from? And why did his mouth now seem to be on autopilot?

Hearing the right answer, and with such confidence from lowly Amby, Mr. Troubar's eyes grew as big as soccer balls in surprise. He held his breath for what seemed like ages… Then, he dropped onto the floor; speechless!

A couple of students started to snicker quietly at seeing their mean teacher suddenly dumbfounded. But their attention was quickly pulled back to Amby as he continued with his answer.

"Every thousand has a coma to separate the thousand and the hundred."

"One thousand thousand is a million."

"One thousand million is a billion."

"One thousand billion or one million million is a trillion."

"One thousand trillion or one million billion is a quadrillion."

"One thousand quadrillion or one million trillion is a quintillion."

"One thousand quintillion or one million quadrillion or one billion trillion is a sextillion. That is, one followed by twenty-one zeros."

Amby kept talking autonomously as additional information invisibly scrolled in front of him. His teacher, who had managed to stagger to his feet, was now sitting in his chair and gripping the seat like it was a life preserver on the Titanic. Even the students in the back could see his cheeks puffed out like a squirrel cramming in a full winter's worth of acorns.

"Tell me the value of ten billion three million plus three billion ten million!" Mr. Troubar further commanded Amby.

"Sir. It's thirteen billion thirteen million. There are nine digits after thirteen for the billion, and there are six digits after thirteen for the million."

"Is there any decimal point for the number?" A livid Mr. Troubar bellowed at Amby.

"No and yes, sir. If yes, it's just one or infinite zeros after the decimal point, meaning there is no value more or less than the whole number."

$$\begin{aligned} & 10{,}003{,}000{,}000.00000000 \\ + \ & 3{,}010{,}000{,}000.00000000 \\ = \ & 13{,}013{,}000{,}000.00000000 \end{aligned}$$

There was bedlam in the classroom. What on earth was going on with Amby? Some kids laughed out loud, feeling so excited at the astonishing win from such a dunce. It served Mr. Troubar right for trying to abase his student instead of helping him get smarter! Maybe what Mr. Troubar really needed was to be shown up more often.

Some, on the other hand, couldn't figure out how Amby had become a math wizard overnight. Math was never his forte, his parents were almost illiterate and so poor that they definitely could not afford a tutor for him. His younger sister was barely learning to add up numbers bigger than ten. So, who could have helped him? Had he found Aladdin's magic lamp?

The smart kids in the class were sure that Amby was cheating. They had lived their lives for more than two quinquenniums, and they knew no one got to be so learned overnight. Amby couldn't have osmosed all the Math books the night before to be so brilliant today. But, but, but... Where was the proof? There was no evidence that Amby was cheating. The whole time, the whole class had been riveted on Amby and they could see that there was nothing in his hands, on his desk or on the wall around the chalkboard with its ginormous number. And while Amby was not the smartest kid in school, he was a kind and honest boy, who always admitted when he was wrong and did his best to fix his mistakes. But whatever was up with Amby's serendipity, the kids could only sit back and enjoy both their friend's transmogrification and Mr. Troubar's flummoxed expression.

Concurrently, Amby was having exactly the same

thoughts as his friends, but he wasn't about to question his new found success. At this moment, he was the center of attention for the best reasons! Even though he was always humble and cared more about the work he did than any superficial praise, he couldn't resist the temptation to enjoy the admiration of his classmates.

Something clicked inside and he was suddenly positive that today was the day he would overcome the disdain that Mr. Troubar had held for him all year. Today was the day when his classmates would see him anew, a star on the pitch and in the classroom. Amby couldn't believe the improbable marvelousness of it all. From this day forth, the sky was the limit; he was ready to realize his dreams. He would break the cycle of being poor and miserable like generations of his families had been. He was sure that Math and soccer were the sure way for him to create a brighter future for himself and his family!

Mr. Troubar was exactly on the opposite spectrum. His head felt like a punching bag getting hammered at from all directions.

No matter the discomfort, Mr. Troubar was not the one to give in so easily. He thought to himself, 'Just a week ago, this half-wit had been incapable of learning anything new in class; as if his brain was hard as granite and not plastic like science had shown. Out of the blue, he turned in homework with perfect and precise answers, for which I had to give him an A+, which I'd never done! And today he's suddenly one of the brightest kids and is humiliating me, the maven of Math, in my own classroom. I don't know what kind of skullduggery he's using, but it ends now!'

After a brief moment to compose himself, Mr. Troubar was fully primed for his next attack.

"What ways can be used to express a value less than a whole number?" he lashed out, trying to suppress the air bubbling in his cheeks and belly.

"Fractions and percentages, sir!" Amby responded loudly.

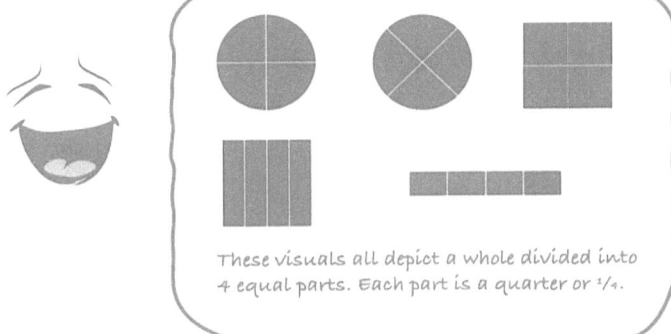

These visuals all depict a whole divided into 4 equal parts. Each part is a quarter or ¹/₄.

That was enough, thought Mr. Troubar. With his four years of professional training in Math and three years in Psychology, there was no way he had misjudged this nincompoop. He needed to make an example out of Amby and make him pay for trying to cheat in his class.

Unrelentingly, Mr. Troubar barked out "What is a fraction?"

"A fraction is a part of a whole number; it is written as one number over another. A third or one over three (1/3); a quarter or one over four (1/4); are both examples of fractional numbers." Amby answered calmly.

Without pause, Amby expounded. "However, sir. There are times when fractions represent more than a whole number, as well. I like this part of Math. There are rules and non-rules, or exceptions. This is where the concept of Improper Fractions comes into play. In Improper Fractions, the numerator has higher value than the denominator. It's not wrong to write number this way, but it's better to make Improper Fractions proper by converting them to Mixed Fractions. For example, twenty-seven over four should be written as six and three quarters."

$$\frac{27}{4} = \frac{24+3}{4} = \frac{24}{4} + \frac{3}{4}$$

$$= 6\,\frac{3}{4}$$

A quick way to convert this improper fraction is knowing 4x7=28, so there must be 6 as the whole number and 3 over 4 as the fraction.

Taking his indignation up another notch, and with his cheeks puffed out as if the squirrel were saving acorns for a decade of winters, the Math teacher probed "What is a percentage?"

"A percentage is another way to express a value less than a whole number. Percent means a hundred, so instead of saying a quarter, or one fourth (1/4), or zero point two five (0.25), we can say twenty five percent (25%). That is, we multiply the decimal number by a hundred and then add the word PERCENT."

Fraction	Decimal	Percentage
1/10	0.10	10%
1/8	0.125	12.5%
1/4	0.25	25%
1/2	0.50	50%
3/4	0.75	75%
4/5	0.80	80%
1/1	1.00	100%

A fraction is another way to represent division task.
1/10 means one divided by ten, which equals 0.1

Mr. Troubar couldn't stand any longer. No more disgrace from this simpleton. This was HIS class to teach, not Amby's.

Oblivious to Mr. Troubar's ire, Amby went on "And just like fractions, percentages can express values more than a whole as well. This is often used when we compare the growth or increase of a value over a period of time. For instance, today I have said about 2,020 words compared with my usual 20 words in your classes, an increase of 2,000 words, which is 100 times or 10,000% more from my baseline verbosity. Wow, I can work with big numbers. Math is suddenly as easy as ABC to me, sir!"

Fun fact – within the human body, physical changes can cause chemical changes, and chemical changes can manifest outwardly. Case in point, the angst created by being shown up by this miserable-know-nothing had built up to the point that Mr. Troubar's skin had turned a lurid shade of red as his blood began to boil. And his voice shot up a whole octave as his throat muscles contracted. "Tell me the value of a third plus three fourths!" he howled like a wolf baying at the moon.

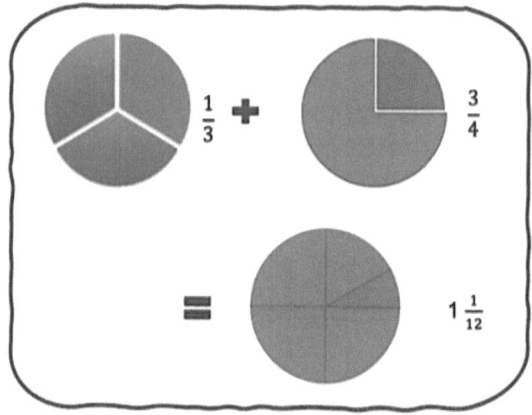

"A whole and one twelfth, sir. One third is actually a quarter and one twelfth (because there are three twelfths in each quarter or four twelfths in each third,) plus three quarters. Improperly that is thirteen twelfths, and thus a proper whole and one twelfth."

Now sounding like a steaming tea kettle, the Math teacher squealed "Tell me the product of one sixth times three fifths!"

"It's three thirtieths or a tenth, sir!"

"Are you sure? How do you explain the rule that

multiplication is actually repeated addition in this case?"

"Certainly sir. One six of one fifth is one thirtieth. There are three fifths so we add three of each one thirtieth together to arrive at three thirtieths. This is computation of a value less than a whole number, so we don't see the repeated addition of a whole number but of a fraction. The same rule applies to numbers of any nature. Multiplication is repeated addition."

$$\frac{1}{6} \times \frac{3}{5} = \left[\frac{1}{6} \times \frac{1}{5}\right] \times 3$$
$$= \frac{1}{\underset{10}{30}} \times \frac{3}{1} = \frac{1}{10}$$

* Multiplication is always repeated addition.
* Simplify a fraction by dividing both the numerator and denominator by the Largest Common Factor.

"What is the quotient of one sixth divided by one half!" he wailed like a banshee hunting for lost souls.

"Two sixths or a third, sir!"

"How come you divided one sixth and you had a bigger quotient?"

"Sir, because one sixth divided by one half means looking for how many halves in one sixth. Since there are three 1/6s in one half, the quotient is 1/3 of one half in 1/6. This explains why when we flip the divisor and multiply it with the dividend, we can get the same result, 1/6 ÷ 1/2 = 1/6 x 2/1 = 2/6 or 1/3."

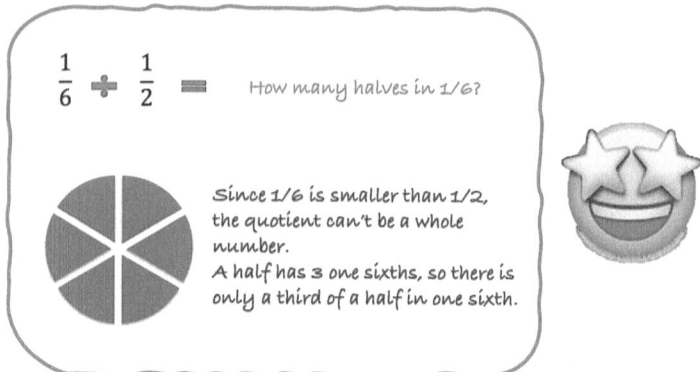

"How about 3/18 + 5/27, tell me the result of this sum." Mr. Troubar drew in a breath of relief as he came up with this tricky problem. Just finding the common denominator, not even solving the problem, for these two fractions was enough to cause his peers splitting migraines. He was sure this would undo the boy.

"Sir, please give me a minute." Amby asked.

'Ha-ha, it would take you millions of minutes to figure this out, boy.' Mr. Troubar could taste sweet victory as his rage started to subside.

"Sir, the result is 19/54." The soccer player responded with confidence.

"Nice guess. Now explain to me all the steps."

"Sir, I prime-factored the denominator of each fraction, 18 = 3 x 3 x 2 and 27 = 3 x 3 x 3. So, to convert both to the same denominator, I need to multiply 3/18 with 3 and 5/27 with 2, resulting in 9/54 + 10/54 = 19/54."

$$\frac{3}{18} + \frac{5}{27} = \frac{3}{3 \times 3 \times 2} + \frac{5}{3 \times 3 \times 3}$$

$$= \frac{3 \times 3}{3 \times 3 \times 2 \times 3} + \frac{5 \times 2}{3 \times 3 \times 3 \times 2} = \frac{19}{54}$$

Least Common Multiple (LCM) is a powerful way to find the common denominator when computing fractions. And the best method to find LCM is to prime-factor each denominator then cross multiply each fraction with only the **different prime factor**.

Mr. Troubar's mind raced. 'My goodness. His computation is clean and neat as salmon sliced by the best Japanese chef. How come he didn't just multiply 3/18 with 27 and 5/27 with 18 like I always taught them?' And suddenly the frenzy that had been wracking the inside of his body turned him into a human volcano on the verge of erupting; steam was pouring out of his ears, nose and mouth. As he tumbled to the floor, he begged of his students "I'm so thirsty, please give me some water!"

As he lay flat on his back before the class, it was clear to the students that Mr. Troubar wouldn't be able to drink from the mug on his desk. Luckily, Sriny had mistakenly grabbed his baby brother's bottle in his haste to get ready for school this morning. He tossed it down to Mr. Troubar to suckle as his classmates rushed around like the Three Stooges, trying to find more liquid for their incapacitated instructor. Predictably, water flowed across the floor and drenched the teacher rather than making it into his mouth.

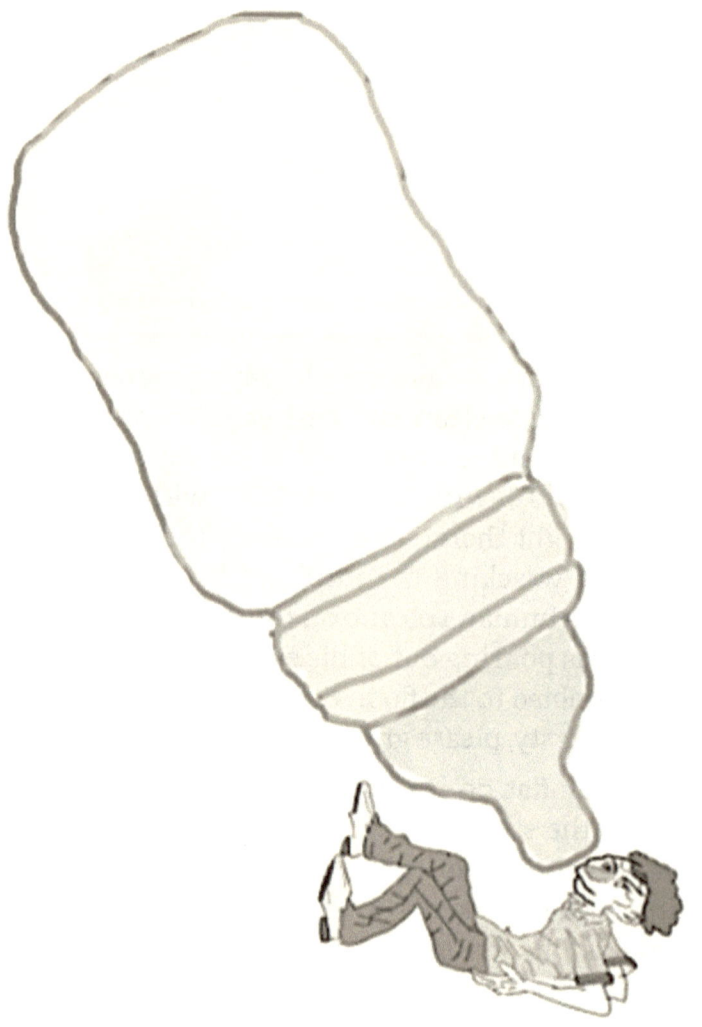

As the cool water hit Mr. Troubar, more steam spewed forth. And now, having finished off the little bit of juice in the bottle, the steam began to fill up the bottle instead. Growing like some weird Macy's parade balloon, the rubber bottle was now ten times bigger than the teacher and had taken up the whole front of the classroom. Before it could grow more and trap them in the classroom, Sriny swiftly mobilized the students to grab the bottle and yanked it away from their pitiful lecturer. Whew! Exhaled the children. Crisis averted.

Battered but not beaten, Mr. Troubar lurched to his feet, took the wacky bottle of hot air to the window, and ripped at the nipple to send it caroming off of the trees around the school like some odd game of pinball. With the pressure inside his body now vented, and ignoring the lifesaving heroics of his class, he once again assailed Amby with his mathematical prowess.

"Which is greater, three hundred forty-five or three hundred forty-four point three eight seven five three seven eight nine five zero seven four five eight seven three nine four five seven eight seven three?" That crazy decimal number was so long there was no way Amby would solve it because a majority of his students thought the longer the decimal number, the bigger it was.

"We compare numbers from left to right, sir. Since five ones are greater than four ones, three hundred forty-five is greater."

345 = 345.00 = 345.00000000000000000

345 > 344.3875378950745873945787 3
because 345 = 345.0000000000000000000000000
       344.3875378950745873945787 3
5 ones is greater than 4 ones so 345 is greater.
However long the decimal part is, it's still less than one whole.

344.3875378950745873945787 3 is less than
344.3875378950746873945787 3
because when comparing from Left to Right (same as
comparing Whole Numbers, 5 <6 even though all other digits
are the same.

The teacher took a deep breath as he thought to himself 'Okay Mr. Smartypants. I don't know how you've mastered Elementary Math, so let's try Middle School Math on for size!' With his new attack plan arranged he demanded: "What is the value of positive two plus negative four?"

Amby startled at this unexpected challenge, but then proceeded apace. "First, we take negative two to zero out positive two, then we will have negative two left. The result is negative two, sir!"

"What? I've never taught any of you how to compute with negative numbers. Is someone in the class helping you?"

The visuals were still in front of Amby's eyes, but the logic of the math was making sense now and he wasn't having to read it verbatim anymore. "It's elementary logic, sir. If I stand up the number line and put it in a big lake, placing zero at the surface of the water, its surface becomes a Mirror Line. Negative numbers are simply a reflection of positive numbers. When working with the two numbers above and below zero, I try to offset them by using the Mirror Line as the guide."

"How about positive two minus negative four?" The Math teacher couldn't resist an evil laugh because the double negative rule always confounded his sixth-grade students.

"Positive six, sir." Amby answered without so much as a blink. "Subtraction in nature is computing a distance on the number line. There are two units on the positive side and there are four units on the negative side, so the distance is six units in total."

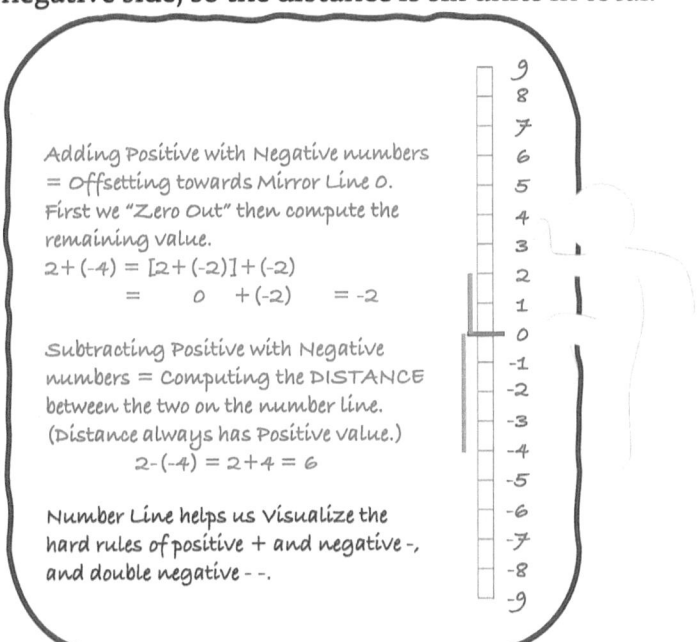

Adding Positive with Negative numbers = Offsetting towards Mirror Line 0. First we "Zero Out" then compute the remaining value.
$$2 + (-4) = [2 + (-2)] + (-2)$$
$$= 0 + (-2) = -2$$

Subtracting Positive with Negative numbers = Computing the DISTANCE between the two on the number line. (Distance always has Positive value.)
$$2 - (-4) = 2 + 4 = 6$$

Number Line helps us visualize the hard rules of positive + and negative -, and double negative - -.

"Amby, you chea........" Mr. Troubar couldn't finish what he wanted to say because of a lack of proof, and such false accusations would get him skinned alive by Principal Fraubaumgartnerfreud. While Amby's elegantly simple description is something Mr. Troubar would have to remember for teaching his older students, his immense ego would never let him admit that to Amby. Instead, like a Pitbull holding on to his favorite stuffed toy, he would never give up until he had completely demeaned Amby.

"Find the negation of negative five for me, Amby!" he announced stridently.

"Negation of negative…" sounded confusing at first, but the soccer player knew which word belonged to which part of information. The first word "negation" meant the opposite of any number. The second word "negative" was the adjective of the noun "five," negative five or minus five was written as "-5" in Math. On the number line, the opposite value of a positive number was the number itself reflected via the mirror at zero, with the size of "-". In other words, a negative value was the opposite of a positive value and vice versa. With that reasoning, he could draw a conclusion that "negation of negative 5" would be looking for the opposite value of -5 on the other side of the number line across 0, or -(-5) was actually positive 5. 'Aha, if I think of Negation as Reflection of a value on the other side of 0, the math is easy peasy!'

"It's Positive Five, sir!!!" Amby spoke loudly with his upmost assurance.

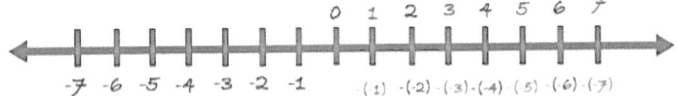

Negating a number means looking for the opposite value of a number over the "mirror" Zero. Hence, negating 1 gives us the value of -1 and negating (-7) gives us the value of -(-7) or 7.

Mr. Troubar could feel the heat and pressure rising inside of him again, but he would not admit defeat, so he pushed forward to find some last way to take this child down. "Amby, where do you see something similar to the number line you were talking about?"

"The Coordinates line, sir. And also on the soccer pitch."

'D*** this kid.' Fumed Mr. Troubar. "How do you know which one is the x coordinate and which one is the y coordinate?"

"Sir. If I stand up the Coordinates, X would be how eXpress my body by spreading my arms wide. And Y would be when I look up at the sky and ask the big question WHY?."

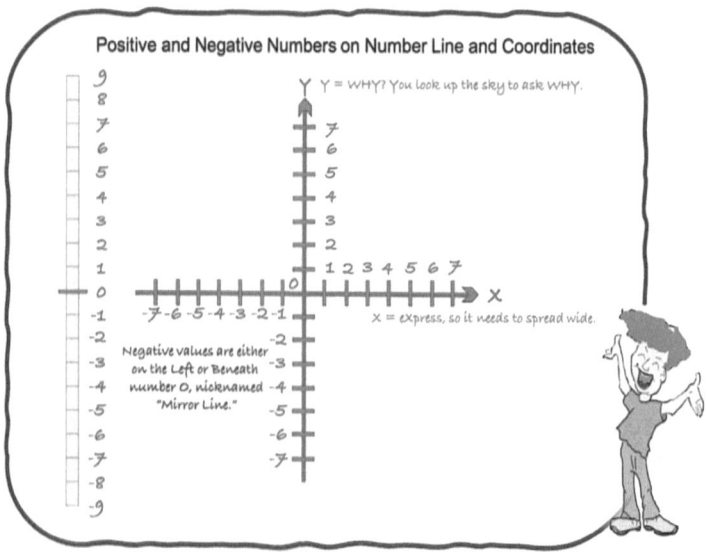

Mr. Troubar was done; his patience had gone, along with any more questions. This mathematical moron had turned into a prodigy with positively prosaic pronouncements that made him look like the dullard. Somebody must have helped Amby, but there was nothing to see except Amby calmly looking him straight in the eyes. He clenched his mouth shut to restrain his rage and closed his eyes in an attempt to discern some possible explanation.

The kids latched onto his actions as a possible sign of defeat and began talking amongst themselves. With no one to rein them in, the chaos of a gaggle of juveniles abruptly escalated into a full-on war of words as they started debating what had happened in class. The teachers of nearby classrooms had to pause their lessons because the roar from Mr. Troubar's room was like a jumbo jet trying to take off from inside their school.

While there was no lack of schadenfreude in the room, the children were also animated in their chatter about the events and reignited their prior debate. Did Amby really know everything by heart or was he using subterfuge to glean the answers from somewhere or someone? There still wasn't anything to evince guilt, so how could they prove to themselves and their friends that Amby was legit? Math class had suddenly become a Forensic Science class.

Meanwhile, Amby sat calmly amongst this hurricane of chatter. To him, it was like the roar of the crowd when the game winning goal was scored in the last minute of the World Cup. He was so happy; much happier than he'd ever felt in his whole life. He always wanted to be smart with Math, but he truly loved being out on the green pitch, where his thoughts and movement were unconstrained. In class, he felt confined by the tiny desk, forced to stare at the board, and exhausted with endless writing on a piece of paper like some medieval torture for his fingers and eyes.

But now, if felt like he had started a new chapter in his life. He couldn't figure out why he was chosen to be the recipient of such a wonderful gift, but the serendipity of it was something he would capitalize on. Tonight, after helping his parents with dinner, he would sit down at the table and focus on his studies. Even though he had started out class just reading the words from the floating screen, he gradually came to truly comprehend what he was saying and started getting ahead of the screen. He understood Math! For REAL! Today, he grasped how cool numbers and logic can be. It was like soccer for his brain; so much movement of ideas and postulations going back and forth until he scored a goal by coming up with the answer. On top of that, he loved looking cool among his friends and no longer being the slowest kid on the block. He felt like a Prime Number; indivisible so long as he believed in himself. No more excuses, no more failure. He knew he would succeed at math and he would change his life, and that of his whole family as well.

Within the classroom, as the kids continued unabated and Amby was a stoic island of Zen tranquility, Mr. Troubar seethed at his desk and started to glow red with resentment. The heat from Mr. Troubar coupled with the hot air from the kids was turning the environment of the classroom into a pressure chamber. Even though ears started to pop from the compression of gasses contained within the walls of the room, no one seemed to notice or care. Just when it seemed the windows must surely shatter, there came a knock at the door.

And then it happened.

Whomever had come to check on the disruptive class turned the latch to open the door and all heck broke loose. Breaking the seal of the room let the pent-up miasma of curiosity and rage explode out into the hall with such a force that it created a minor vacuum in the classroom. The sudden release of pressure took the exterior force off of Mr. Troubar, which caused his constrained indignation to distend him into the human approximation of a puffer fish. But there's only so much stretch in human skin and the body has efficient mechanisms of expelling gasses, which was exactly what occurred, in a most noxious manner.

With methane displacing oxygen in the room, the kids vomited out the hole left behind when door had blown off its hinges, flowing down the halls like a tsunami amongst the canyons of a city.

Fortunately, Amby, Sriny, and some other brave kids kept their wits, held their breath, and managed to get to the incapacitated Mr. Troubar. Grabbing at any appendage they could, they managed to drag the teacher into the hallway just as the school nurse, after fighting her way through the anarchy in the halls, arrived at the scene.

◆ ◆ ◆

Whew! Such a day for the kids! What a day for Mr.

Troubar!

The school was abuzz.

Who had caused such panic at the school?

Was Amby really the best at math now?

Had Mr. Troubar really floated around before popping?

Why did the whole school smell like the cafeteria after chili day?

What was going on at the sleepy old Dozzaff?

Nobody knew the answers to these questions. But everybody could feel that something had changed in the school and they were all curious and anxious about what would happen next.

CHAPTER TWO
GOING WILD

In the week following that fateful day, Mr. Troubar was very reserved. He delivered his lessons in an even flatter monotone than before, which didn't seem possible, and he spent more time looking at the board than at the class. Instead of verbally quizzing the kids, as a pretext to humiliate them, he just had the class turn in written exercises. But something in Mr. Troubar's eyes let the kids know that he was plotting something.

Amby continued to do exceptionally well in class and he had become a minor celebrity outside of class. During break time, some of his friends would ask him challenging math problems and others asked him to tutor them. Being a good egg as always, Amby gave freely of his time and newfound skills to help his classmates. They immediately came to realize that Amby wasn't a cheat; the clarity and exactness of his answers could only come from someone who had mastered the subject. Sometimes he would draw diagrams to help get his point across, but most of the time his words painted a picture in the minds of his compatriots. The visuals he had seen that fateful day had never reappeared, but the logic and the flow remained etched in his memory. As a result, he barely gave any thought to the mystery of the floating images.

Friday arrived and everybody was in a good mood and looking forward to a weekend away from the pressures of school. As Mr. Troubar strode confidently into Math class with a large sack of something colorful in his hand, the kids speculated that the dullness of the past week was about to end.

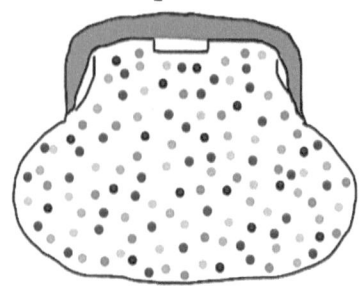

Barely setting his bag down on the desk, Mr. Troubar launched into his lecture. Using his *'I'm going to pick on you because I'm smarter and better than you'* voice, he asked the little boy who was hunched over his desk at the far side of the classroom, "Trinny, recite to me the two times table."

Trinny wasn't stupid, but his math performance was inconsistent. Sometimes he scored very well, sometimes he got the worst grade. He loved stories and being creative and had a hard time with the cold rationality of numbers and formulas. For him, if there wasn't any E, there was no motion in his thoughts. Trinny's world centered around the "Emotions" he felt when writing or being lost in a great story; hence he spent his time in accordance with his own rationale.

Lost in the story he was furtively reading under his desk, he was unresponsive until Mr. Troubar tapped him on the shoulder and repeated the request "Trinny, tell me the two times table."

Clearly startled, Trinny leapt to his feet, collected himself quickly and started spewing out the two times table, "two, four, six, eight, ten, twelve…!" It was the easiest one, because it was super easy to add two more to the last number. It's also the same as reciting all the even numbers, with the tens moved up one more every time the ones rolled over to a zero. Trinny, lost in his thoughts and feeling so passionate about his skill with 2's, kept on reciting the two times table. "2 times 97 are 194; 2 times 98 are 196; 2 times 99 are 198, 2 times 100 are 200, 2 times 101 are 202."

"That's enough." Mr. Troubar stopped him with a dismissive waive of his hand. "Clearly that was much too easy for you. So let's try random combinations and answer me as fast as you can. What are 3 times 8?

"2 times 8 are 16, plus one more 8 equals... 26 minus 2... equals 24. It's 24, sir!"

"Don't use addition for the times table, just tell me the result right away." Even though multiplication was actually repeated addition, Mr. Troubar wanted to force the kids to memorize the tables by heart like he did, and not take any shortcuts.

"What are 7 x 8, Trinny?"

"It's... 56, sir." Trinny paused a bit before saying the result. He still needed to use addition to compute the math. He memorized the square of all numbers from 1-12 but remembering every piece of every times table was too much work for rote learning. Knowing 8 x 8 was the same as 8 squared or 64, he then subtracted one 8 to get to 7 x 8, that equaled 56.

1 x 1	2
2 x 2	4
3 x 3	9
4 x 4	16
5 x 5	25
6 x 6	36
7 x 7	49
8 x 8	64
9 x 9	81
10 x 10	100
11 x 11	121
12 x 12	144

It's good to memorize the Squares and 2, 5, 10 times tables. The rest can be computed based on those times table.

There is no need to memorize all the times tables.

- 2 times table = doubling
- 3 times table can be computed by using 2 or 4 times tables.

E.g.: $3 \times 7 = (2+1) \times 7 = (4-1) \times 7$
$= 2 \times 7 + 1 \times 7 = 4 \times 7 - 1 \times 7 = 21$.

- $2 \times 2 = 4$, $2 \times 2 \times 2 = 8$. So when working with 4 times table, we can double 2 times, with 8 times table we can double 3 times.

E.g.: $4 \times 9 = 2 \times (2 \times 9) = 2 \times 18 = 36$.
$8 \times 9 = 2 \times [2 \times (2 \times 9)] = 2 \times 2 \times 18 = 2 \times 36 = 72$.

- $6 = 5 + 1 = 2 \times 3$ so we can work with 6 times table using 5 or 2 and/or 3 times table.

E.g.: $6 \times 8 = 5 \times 8 + 1 \times 8 = 2 \times 8 + 3 \times 8 = 48$

- $7 = 5 + 2 = 6 + 1 = 8 - 1$, so we can work with 7 times table using 2, 5, 6, 8 times tables.
- $5 \times 2 = 10$ so we can double 5 to use 10 times table, or halve 10 to use 5 times table.

E.g.: $5 \times 9 = (10 \div 2) \times 9 = 90 \div 2 = 45$.

- 8, 9, 11, 12 are close to 10, so use the 10 times table as the landmark.

E.g.: $8 \times 7 = 10 \times 7 - 2 \times 7 = 70 - 14 = 56$
$9 \times 9 = 10 \times 9 - 1 \times 9 = 81$
$12 \times 11 = 10 \times 11 + 2 \times 11 = 110 + 22 = 132$

"Better. What are 5 x 9?"

"It's... 45." Trinny mumbled the "90 then half" part. He ac

tually doubled 5 to 10 then multiplied 10 with 9 to get to 90, then he halved it to 45. He wanted to be a good boy today, so he only let his teacher hear what he wanted to hear.

"Good work, Trinny. Please take a seat!" said Mr. Troubar as he walked back to the front of the room. At his desk, he reached into his bag and promptly inflated seven balloons and let them drift up to the ceiling. The class was
perplexed at what Mr. Troubar was doing. It was a welcome sight to see him bring color and fun into

the classroom. And even though they still didn't fully trust his intentions, they relaxed a bit and opened themselves to listen to the Math teacher.

Mr. Troubar turned his attention to another student. "Mathew, please recite the 12 times table." Even though he had asked in a softer voice, there a hard edge to it that signified he wasn't relenting.

Mathew was a bunch of nerves. He was scribbling something with his pencil. Math was never his forte. He could imagine beautiful landscapes and great adventures and sketch them out in a matter of minutes. But numbers slowed him down, making him feel like an abject loser among his friends. The fear of losing face pushed him into a downward shame spiral of dodging math whenever he could, but then other days he felt even worse when he could not answer Math questions. It was like Math was a bully who would shove him to the ground and steal his lunch money; basically the thing he wanted to avoid at all costs.

He had to respond to Mr. Troubar's direct request, though. He was about to start his reply when something popped up in front of his eyes. It was transparent and it shifted around as his eyes moved, but it was clearly only visible to him. Whatever was happening, he was seeing the 12 times table floating in front of him, with an explanation he had never seen. So he started to read it off. "Sir, 12 times 1 equals 12. 12 times 2 equals 20..."

"Balderdash! What nonsense are you spouting?" The Math teacher lost his cool. He was too impatient to wait for the boy to realize his error.

The butterflies in Mathew's stomach started churning intensely as he picked up "... plus 4 equals 24, sir. Sorry it took time for me to finish my sentence. 12 times 3 equals 30 plus 6 equals... 36. 12

12 x 1	10x1 + 2x1	12
12 x 2	10x2 + 2x2	24
12 x 3	10x3 + 2x3	36
12 x 4	10x4 + 2x4	48
12 x 5	10x5 + 2x5	60
12 x 6	10x6 + 2x6	72
12 x 7	10x7 + 2x7	84
12 x 8	10x8 + 2x8	96
12 x 9	10x9 + 2x9	108
12 x 10	10x10 + 2x10	120
12 x 11	10x11 + 2x11	132
12 x 12	10x12 + 2x12	144

Since 12 = 10 + 2, we first times the multiplier with 10 then add a double of it. Memorizing without understanding the logic is tough for everybody.

times 4 equals 40 plus 8 equals... 48."

"I need you to enumerate the times table, not to use addition to calculate it on the fly!"

The boy started once again. "Yes sir, I will try my best. 12 times 5 equals...," he paused as the visuals threw a large SSSHHH! to remind him to internalize the calculation in his head before saying only the answer Mr. Troubar expected. Just a glance at the table made everything fall into place for Matthew and he recognized that *not* using addition for the times table wasn't at all sensible. Just last week, Mr. Troubar commanded Amby to explain why multiplication was repeated addition, so why wasn't it appropriate today? However, Mathew didn't want to argue.

"... equals 60. 12 times 6 equals seventy.... two. 12 times 7 equals eighty... four. 12 times 8 equals ninety... six. 12 times 9 equals one hundred and eight. 12 times 10 equals a hundred twenty. 12 times 11 equals a hundred thirty-two. 12 times 12 equals a hundred forty-four." As he finished, Matthew clasped his hands together on the desk and quietly thanked whom ever gave him the magic table that helped him through the challenge.

As the Math teacher took a moment to process Matthew's correctness, he blew more balloons to defray his peevishness. He figured that Mathew's measured responses meant he was still using addition to calculate the next item in the 12 times table, so he would ask him something totally different to throw him off.

"Why does 12 times 10 equal 120? Why is there a zero after number 12?" "Sir, because 12 x 10 = 12 + 12 + 12 + 12 + 12 +

12 + 12 + 12 + 12 + 12 = 24 + 24 + 24 + 24 + 24 = 48 + 2 + 48 + 2 + 20 = 120. Whenever we multiply any number with ten, it means we add that number 10 times together, the result always has a zero at the end. Zero here means 10 times more." The visuals quickly showed him what he needed to tackle the sudden request.

"Tell me the result of 12 x 5 immediately!" Mr. Troubar commanded.

"It's 60, sir."

"Not bad. Did you memorize it?" The teacher further queried.

"No, I computed it, sir. 12 x 5 is a half of 12 x 10 because 5 is a half of 10. So, I just calculated 12 x 10 first, then I halved the result of 120 to arrive at 60." Mathew swiftly followed the process that the visuals showed him.

"How about 12 x 9, tell me the result right away!"

"108 sir."

"Did you memorize it?"

"No sir, I computed it too. 12 x 9 is one 12 less than 12 x 10 because 9 is one less than 10, so I computed 12 x 10 first then subtracted one 12 from 120 to get to 108."

Mathew didn't realize that his explanation gave some clue for Mr. Troubar to escalate to even trickier questions.

"How about 12 x 8?

"96, sir."

"Did you memorize it?

"No sir. I computed it as well."

"Did you subtract anything from 120 or 12 x 10?"

"No sir. I multiply 8 with 10 to get 80, then I double 8 to get 16. 80 plus 16 equals 96."

'Hmmmm. This boy really knows how to do Math in different ways.' Mr. Troubar thought as he paused to blow some more balloons before he continued. "You seem to like doubling and halving. Let's have some fun with them. What is the product of twenty-five thousand four hundred thirty-five (25,435) and two?" He had to cover his smirk after stating the big number to the little boy.

The class let out a little groan at their teacher's quiz. But they also covertly crossed their fingers in hopes that Matthew could show him up like Amby had done.

"It's fifty thousand eight hundred seventy (50,870), sir." The secretive visual instantly came into play to save Mathew again.

"Go ahead and explain how you did it!"

"I double the number from left to right. First, I double twenty-five (25) to get fifty (50). This is the thousands. Next, I double four hundred. Again, I don't worry about the hundred placements, just work with 4 times 2 to get 8 and add the hundred in later. Doubling 35 is easy. I can double 30 first then double 5 and add them together, but it takes longer. So, I save time by doubling 35 right away; it's 70. In the end, I add everything together. It's fifty thousand, eight hundred seventy."

A bright idea crept into Mr. Troubar's mind. Doubling digits less than five was easy, because the result of one placement never got to more than 10 to affect the larger placements to the left.

"Tell me the value when you double five hundred ninety-two thousand, five hundred seventy-three (592,573)." He purposely used digits larger than five to dupe the boy.

Mathew was still for a bit as he worked it out and his friends close by could hear him murmuring his thought process. "Six hundred then 12 hundred, minus 16, equals 11 hundred eighty-four. 12 hundred minus 54 equals 11 hundred forty-six."

"It's 1,185,146, sir." he proclaimed exuberantly.

Mr. Troubar blew out 20 balloons in a row!!! The whole classroom was in awe; kids started drumming their desks in concert. Another poor performer had turned into a wunderkind today! He was working with numbers in the millions and yet the class was barely into the thousands in their curriculum.

"Explain it to me, sir."

The class went instantly silent. They had never heard Mr. Troubar address any student with any modicum of respect.

"Sir, I used the method of rounding up and

doubling a cluster of digits instead of one digit at a time. 592 thousand is very close to 600 thousand so I doubled 600 thousand to get to 1200 thousand then subtract the doubling of the 8 thousand difference, that is 16 thousand. The result for the thousands is 1,184 thousand. Then comes the rest. 573 is further away from 600 but still it's easier to round it up to 600 than to 500 or 550 because I used 600 for the thousand already. After doubling it to get to 1200, I subtracted 27 times 2 - that is 54 - to offset the difference for rounding up. The result is 1,146. Now I just add it with 1,184 thousand to arrive at 1,185,146 for the final value." Mathew talked confidently along the with visuals. By the time he spoke the last of the answer, he understood it completely.

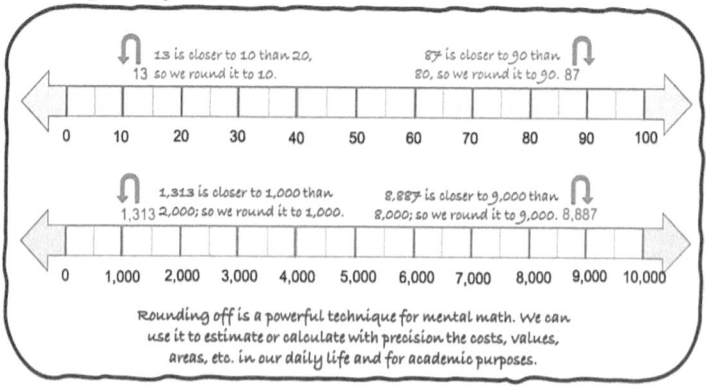

Mr. Troubar always asked his students to line up numbers one on top of the other and compute the addition from right to left using the standard method. It worked very well, but his students needed to write down the answer as they went.

However, this little brainiac not only showed how to do all the math mentally, but also to work from left to right. Mr. Troubar wondered why he hadn't thought of this before and then filed it away in his bag of tricks before coming up with a devilish problem to knock Matthew down a couple of pegs.

"Halve 3,531,157 for me." He purposely used all odd numbers instead of even numbers to make it really tricky.

"It's 1,765,578.5, sir." The boy answered without hesitation. Halving was the same as dividing by 2. All division needed to work from left to right, no issue for him.

Half	Original	Original	Half
3,452,394	6,904,788	6,904,768	3,452,384
8,394,794	16,789,588	16,589,588	8,294,794
34,563,465	69,126,930	69,146,930	34,573,465
1,439,473	2,878,946	2,880,946	1,440,473
839,723	1,679,446	1,779,446	889,723
234,888	469,776	469,886	234,943
455,435	910,870	930,870	465,435
29,474,739	58,949,478	58,951,478	29,475,739
47,498	94,996	97,996	48,998
2,824,759	5,649,518	5,769,518	2,884,759
192,773	385,546	785,546	392,773
9,183,748	18,367,496	18,589,496	9,294,748
29,384	58,768	70,768	35,384
35,346,563	70,693,126	95,693,126	47,846,563

This table illustrates the changes of 1-3 digits in the original numbers that can affect 1-3 digits in the result of halving. (Doubling is multiplying 2 with the numbers in the Half column.

A useful technique is to work in a cluster of digits. Doubling 35,346,563 becomes doubling first 35 million -> 70 million, then 346 thousand -> 692 thousand, finally 563 ones -> 1,126; the end result is 70,693,126.

It looks a bit challenging to work with big numbers at first, but once the brain gets used to it, it will become easy very quickly.

With an inward sigh, Mr. Troubar decided to cut his losses. "You can sit down and rest, Mathew. Thank you."

Even though Matthew had clearly won the

contest, and Mr. Troubar was still being calm and respectful, the class stayed mum as they watched more balloons being inflated and set free into the room. Even if this was not their regular Math class, everybody wished that all of them could be as colorful and enjoyable as today. And they were even more fascinated as to why Mr. Troubar was acting so differently today.

As the Math teacher completed his exhalations, he narrowed his eyes as he found his next victim. "Ghanna, if each student dances 3 hours every day, and there are 24 hours each day; how many hours do 30 groups, each consisting of 30 students dance over the course of 30 years?"

The whole class gasped at the enormity of this word problem; they had never been asked to work something so difficult before. Did Mr. Troubar forget that he wasn't teaching the 7th graders today? All eyes turned to Ghanna.

For a second, Ghanna had the same puzzled look she always got when working with math. However, after a second, she switched her mindset. She was a dancer and this problem was about her, so she did what came naturally to her. She stood up, began to twirl around her desk, and lost herself in delightful day dreams. As she moved, she imagined herself moving from one country to another, dancing in a Japanese Kimono then in an Indian Sari... As her mind opened up to the splendor of the world, she started to see all the important figures lining out, right in front of her eyes. "30 groups x 30 students in each group x 3 hours per day x 365 days in a year x 30 years." Wait a minute, did she need to put in 24 hours a day too? Oh no, that's a trap, just a number thrown in to confuse her; she only needed to care about the 3 hours of dancing each day. So, it's just "30 x 30 x 30 x 3 x 365 or 80,000 times 365 plus 1,000 times 365," she muttered along with the visual. Completing her final twirl, she faced Mr. Troubar and ecstatically shouted "It's 29,565,000 hours, sir!"

Mr. Troubar suddenly went stiff like he had been hit by lightning. He was unprepared for another student to actually succeed and was clearly annoyed. He heaved his body into his chair and filled 50 more balloons with his hot air.

Mr. Troubar finally spoke in a mellow voice. "You now can take a seat, Ghanna. Thank you." His eyes wandered across the classroom, searching for new quarry, when he spotted Trikkie, a kid who loved to eat and used his bulk to bully the other kids.

"Trikkie, you like things very big, right? Tell me the quotient of 42,385 divided by 49!" The Math teacher mandated with a hint of pleasure in his voice.

Smiles erupted on every face in the class except for Trikkie's. Everyone, including Mr. Troubar, felt that it was time for Trikkie to get his comeuppance for being so mean to everyone else just because his was bigger. Trikkie on the other hand, lost his ordinary attitude of being untouchable and burst into a vociferous reaction within a second. He started squirming around at his desk like there were millions of ants in his pants; he clearly wanted to escape, but it was like his butt was transfixed to the chair.

His tears and screaming really annoyed the kids because he was finally doing what he had caused so many others to do before. However, after a couple of minutes of this nonstop suffering, even his victims started feeling sad for him and wished they could help him; no good person enjoys seeing another suffer. Just when everyone thought Trikkie's crying would devolve into a series of jagged hiccups and gasps for air, out of the blue, he regained his composure and squeaked out "Sir, it's 865!"

Eyes bulged and mouths dropped open. Trikkie's pronouncement, and the correct one at that, astonished the whole class. Mr. Troubar was irked. "How did you do it?", he demanded to know.

"I divided 42,385 by 7 to get to 6,055, then I divided it by another 7 to get to 865. I am smart and this problem is too easy for me."

Mental Math made easy!

Number	Factors		
49	7	7	
60	10	2	3
40	10	2	2
42	2	3	7
75	3	5	5
45	3	3	5
8	2	2	2
27	3	3	3
125	5	5	5
21	3	7	
28	2	2	7
90	10	3	3

- Factoring is powerful for mental math. Instead of dividing or multiplying with big numbers, use factoring to work with simple and/or single digit numbers.
  E.g.: $42,385 \div 49 = 42,385 \div 7 \div 7 = 6,055 \div 7 = 865$
  $35 \times 21 = 35 \times 7 \times 3 = 245 \times 3 = 735$
- 10, 100, 1000 and multiples of these are efficient in simplifying the math problems.
  E.g.: $34,743,780 \div 60$ is the same as $3,474,378 \div 6$, the same as $3,474,378 \div 2 \div 3 = 1,737,189 \div 3 = 579,063$
- When using factors, make sure to pick the easy factor to start with.
  E.g.: $18 \times 14 = 18 \times 7 \times 2$. Between 7 and 2, let's start with 7 because it's easy to multiply a smaller number, 18, with 7 then double the result than double the original 18 to bigger number 36 then multiply it with 7.
- Factoring doesn't work all the time because there are many prime numbers. In that case, try Rounding off method.
  E.g.: $14 \times 19 = 14 \times (20 - 1) = 14 \times 20 - 14 \times 1 = 266$

Offended by his cocky attitude, Mr. Troubar gave him a real thinker. "What is the quotient of 60 into 34,743,780."

The floating screen that had helped Trikkie appeared again. It flashed the number 579.063 briefly and then disappeared. Luckily, he was fast enough to catch and repeat it "It's five hundred seventy-nine, point zero six three, sir."

"What? I asked you to divide more than thirty million by sixty, and you have only some hundreds as the quotient?"

The visual reappeared, enlarging the dot symbol to reveal it was in fact an itty bitty comma. Then it squirmed around and turned into a goofy face. Trikkie lost his temper and stomped the floor like when someone else got the last piece of pie. Everyone got a good laugh at Trikkie's failure and ensuing tantrum.

Mr. Troubar was enjoying finally being able to lord his mental prowess again and so he kept bamboozling the boy: "What is the square of 105?"

Trikkie sat thinking for a minute; then two; then three; and then four. Four stretched into five minutes and still no visuals appeared to aid him. He closed his eyes to pray, but that didn't help either and he burst into tears again. His continued distress negated the joy the kids had felt earlier at his embarrassment.

Then suddenly he saw 11.025. He didn't read it out right away but spent a second thinking. It's the square of a number larger than 100 so the result needed to be more than a thousand not ten something. He wouldn't be fooled this time.

"It's 11,025, sir." He choked out between swallowing the torrent of tears still streaming down his face.

"How do you get that?

After so much pressure, Trikkie wasn't audacious enough to fib. "I have no idea, sir. The answers just materialized before my eyes; but it was messing with me so that I would give an incorrect answer."

Mental Math made easy!

Square of	Rewrite	Result
45	(50-5)x(40+5)	2025
85	(90-5)x(80+5)	7225
95	(100-5)x(90+5)	9025
115	(120-5)x(110+5)	13225
27	(30-3)x(24-3)	729
47	(50-3)x(44+3)	2209
58	(60-2)x(56+2)	3364
68	(70-2)x(66+2)	4624
99	(100-1)x(98+1)	9801

Please use the method shown on the right to double check these result.

- Rewriting the numbers to compute in the problems is a powerful method for mental math. For squaring, it's also important to pick the right distance from the original numbers to help you work with 10 or multiple of 10.

E.g.: $35^2 = (40-5) \times (30+5) = 40 \times 30 + 5(40-30-5) = 40 \times 30 + 5 \times 5 = 1,200 + 25 = 1,225$

$75^2 = (80-5) \times (70+5) = 80 \times 70 + 5(80-70-5) = 80 \times 70 + 5 \times 5 = 5,600 + 25 = 5,625$

$105^2 = (110-5) \times (100+5) = 110 \times 100 + 5(110-100-5) = 110 \times 100 + 5 \times 5 = 11,000 + 25 = 11,025$

- When the number doesn't end with 5, we can still rewrite it to 10 or multiple of 10. A bit harder for the second number, but it still works very easily.

E.g.: $36^2 = (40-4) \times (32+4) = 40 \times 32 + 4(40-32-4) = 40 \times (30+2) + 4 \times 4 = 1,200 + 80 + 16 = 1,296$

$47^2 = (50-3) \times (44+3) = 50 \times 44 + 3(50-44-3) = 50 \times (40+4) + 3 \times 3 = 2,000 + 200 + 9 = 2,209$

Amby, Trinny, Matthew, and Ghanna made a strangled little sound, fearing that Mr. Troubar would catch on about the secretive illustrations that had helped them learn but also perplex their teacher.

Mr. Troubar strode to Trikkie's desk and walked around it several times, mumbling to himself as he went. The students knew this was abnormal but he was so quiet, no student could figure out what was going on inside his head.

Mr. Troubar finally decided to return to the front of the room. On the way, he saw Keith furiously writing. Even with the cursory glance he got as he passed by, Mr. Troubar could see a desk full of papers and the ones on top seemed to each have a solution for one of the challenges that Mr. Troubar had posed to the students. As he continued forward, his eyebrows scrunched together and he uttered something that went unheard.

As the last of the balloons drifted upwards with the vented ire of Mr. Troubar, he gathered his things and offhandedly dismissed the class just before he vanished into the hallway. Rather than dwell on his odd behavior, the kids jumped up in excitement and started bounding around the room and on the desks to get at the layers of balloons bumping around the space. Kids picked them up, bounced them around, popped them, and had the most fabulous end of the week ever.

Back home, Mr. Troubar was totally different. He was kind of optimistic and in a rush. The balloons were a great idea to help him exorcize his anger and stay calm so that he could carry out his mission perfectly. They also worked as distraction for his other purpose. Nobody had figured out his plan, and with his eagle eyes, he was confident that he was about to find out something critical. Super critical.

The floating numbers Trikkie mentioned and Keith's writings couldn't have been coincidental. Keith was the smartest kid in Dozzaff, and he was a tech nerd as well. Every teacher was baffled at how he knew more than what he was taught at school, especially since his guardian was his older-  than-old grandpa. But that mystery was about to end. Over the past week, he had gone on a shopping spree at all the tech stores in town to gather all the gadgets he needed to spy on the class: 50 miniscule, high-def cameras with cinema quality audio. Using the balloons as decoys, he kept the kids focused on the pretty colors and away from his hidden gadgets.

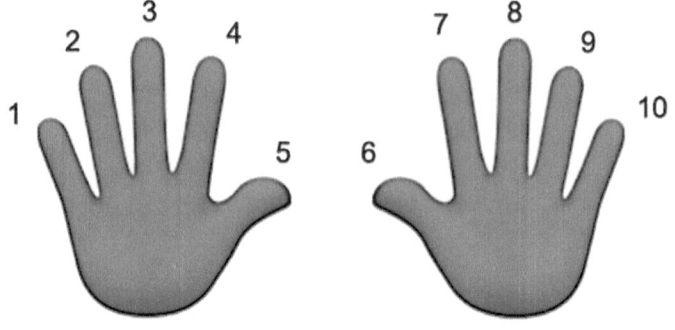

The 10-base can be used for any placements: ones, tens, hundreds, thousands, ten thousands, hundred thousands, millions, and so on...

Mr. Troubar reviewed all of the recordings late into the evening, trying to discern how the kids were cheating. He saw lots of hand movements by the students who were answering his questions, but all he could ascertain was that they used their fingers to do the Math. That was how counting started. Humans used fingers to count from 1 to 10, then to the next 10, ... then to one hundred, then two hundred, and so on. The placement didn't matter. It's all 10-based, for the ones, the tens, the hundreds, the thousands, the ten thousands, ... to the sextillions and so on.

Failing to see anything obvious with the answerers, he zeroed in on Keith to see if he had surreptitiously cast anything towards the eyes of the kids; like with a miniature projector. But there was nothing on Keith's desk but his papers; no little box or the glint of projected light. Nada. All he could see was Keith solving all the problems exactly as his friends had answered. And Keith never turned around or made any signal to indicate he was helping his friends.

Hoping against hope, Mr. Troubar spent a month straight, using up all of his spare time, watching all his recordings over and over again. His Holmesian mission to ferret out the truth of the matter was fruitless and all he had to show for his efforts was bad posture and the eyes of a raccoon.

He would never admit defeat, but it was clearly time to change tactics. Whatever illicit help the students were getting would be discovered and his suspicions would be vindicated in the end.

The next Monday, it was back to business as usual in Mr. Troubar's class. Other than Mr. Troubar looking like he hadn't slept a wink all weekend, it was just a normal, everyday, math class. There were no more balloons or explosions, no more tantrums to shake the walls, as if the last couple of weeks had never happened.

However, the kids couldn't shake what had happened, so they convened at lunchtime to discuss events from the last couple weeks. Topic number one was the furtive images. Since each kid's description of the visual aids lined up with everyone else's, they deduced that they weren't hallucinations. What they didn't get was why someone was helping them to be better at Math on the sly. Just like Mr. Troubar, they had all seen Keith writing during class and the mass of papers on his desk, but he had never tried to help them before. And what did he have to gain by giving them the answers and knowledge through the floating screens? Maybe it was aliens or ghosts of students past or maybe even God. But after hashing this out for several weeks with no definitive answers, the kids lost interest in the question.

Nevertheless, many poor performers had benefitted from seeing the math visually and were excited by the how easy it was to break down the math problems now. With this awakening to the beauty of Math, the kids started to feel more confident and cooler. Just like Amby, they dove into understanding Math, played around with calculating, and performed computations based on the world around them. During break time, instead of running around on the playground, they flung themselves into challenging each other to do division and multiplication using factoring, squaring, halving, and doubling methods. The games went on and on for many days and became progressively more difficult and thought-provoking. Even the shiest kid had become a conjurer of mathematical conundrums. Against all odds, and without any involvement of the teachers, the school suddenly became a hotbed of Math virtuosos. Would pigs be flying next?

One day, Trinny had a wild idea for a fabulous contest. "Let's come up with the grossest Math problems and see who can solve them the quickest!"

There was resounding agreement from the group. This would be so fun; they were never short of revolting ideas.

Ghanna, who loved to put on costumes for her performances, excitedly commenced: "If we make wigs from desiccated flies, how many do we need if the size of each fly is 0.5 cm2, each wig measures 500 cm2, and we need 1 wig each for 100 dancers."

"Vile!!!" the kids howled in disgust. Touching even a single dead fly already made them squeamish; the thought of wearing a wig of them made their skin crawl. Who would even have the nerve to don that headdress?

"500 cm2 x 100 dancers x 0.5 cm2 =?"

"25,000 flies! That's half of 50,000." Blake squealed in triumph. He used to be the quietest boy in the classroom, but not anymore. These days he was very vocal, lively, and ready to engage in conversation with other kids on a variety of topics.

"Bravo for your wonderful idea Ghanna and kudos to Blake for such a rapid solution. Who's next?" Trinny asked.

Mathew's hand shot up and he followed with a no less sickening Math problem. "If we can pick up 20 pieces of dog poop in 15 minutes, how many hours do we need to pick up all of the dog poop for all 300 houses in the neighborhood, each with 40 poops in the yard." As much as kids love their puppies, they exerted the same level of emotion, but on the opposite spectrum, for picking up canine waste. Kids often needed a huge incentive to complete this particular responsibility.

"20 poops in 15 minutes... is 40 in 30 minutes... which is half of 300. It's 150 hours." Bobba answered within a minute. Bobba loved his food and video games, which made him a rotund lazybones. But this brain game was so fun he didn't dare miss out playing with his friends. Knowing 15 minutes was a quarter of an hour, 30 minutes was half of an hour, which was the time needed to pick up all 40 droppings for each household, then 300 houses would need ½ hour each, equaling 150 hours to service the subdivision. He used fractions to convert minutes to hours without having to work a time-consuming computation with minutes. He played with fractions of hours all the time since he loved pizza so much, and a pizza was just like the round clock on his wall at home.

Kids whistled, clapped their hands, and drummed on the benches to cheer for the two winners.

"Bingo. Mathew and Bobba rule!" Trinny declared.

Keith jumped into the game. "If we change our diet to only eat live June bugs for food, how much money could each of us save if we capture 4,000 June bugs from our backyard each day for 2 weeks, provided that, on average, we spend $20 for food per day."

"I'd rather save money by not eating at all than by eating June bugs." Someone shrieked in horror.

"Crunch, crunch, crunch." mimed another kid, warming to the possibility.

The class started throwing ideas out as they thought.

"4,000 bugs x 14 days x $20???"

"Oh no, 4,000 June bugs sounds like a lot. How many do we need per meal? I don't think we'd finish them off in just one day, even if we ate them for all 3 meals plus a couple of snacks."

"How much do June bugs go for at the grocery store?"

"It's $280." Allen, Smock, and Grek answered simultaneously. Smock explained to the others "All that matters is that we're no longer spending $20 a day for 14 days. That's $280 in total." They were all winners for this challenge, of course.

After contemplating for some time, Meggie, the biology nerd who had a predilection for anything microscopic, cleared her throat and queried the group: "Suppose there are 10 million bacteria on each of our fingers. How many bacteria do we swallow when we bite a finger nail or lick food off our fingers, provided that each of us conducts this germy habit 30 times every single day?"

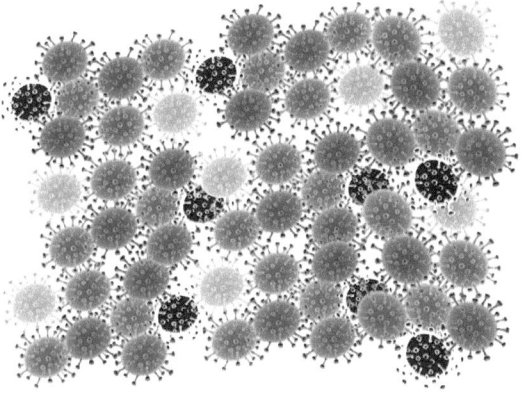

Half of the kids got goose bumps and the other half shivered in disgust. This was the creepiest math challenge yet. After this sickening statistic, who would dare to put their unsanitary fingers anywhere near their mouth anymore? Some kids touched their belly and wondered if it had grown so big because it was holding gazillions of bacteria?

"30 times 10 million. That's 300 million bacteria." mumbled a nervous kid in the back; grossed out that he might be right.

"Correct" said Meggie. "Don't worry. Most of the

bacteria of our biome aren't harmful to us and some of the bacteria even defend us. So even when bacteria from other people or the desks or the dog get into our bodies, there's a low risk it'll hurt us." Meggie tried to allay her classmates' fears. "And the good news is, if you keep washing your hands with soap and drop the bad habit of putting your fingers in your mouth, you'll be fine."

"Meggi, you rocked!" Trinny concluded. Then he whipped around at a rude sound and deleterious smell. "Did somebody just fart?"

"That was me," Grek said. "I apologize for the unseemly notice, but I have an odiferous challenge. Assuming one can propel their body up into outer space by farts alone, how many farts would one need to have enough horsepower to complete the deed?"

"You didn't give us enough information." Ghanna said.

"It's ok, we can look it up." Mathew assured his friends.

Mathew and the kids looked up the information on the internet and were amazed by the results. "A fart can travel 10 feet in a second. That's about 6.82 miles per hour." From there Mathew postulated "I remember seeing that a car traveling at 720 miles per hour needs 15,000 horsepower. So, since a fart can travel at 6.82 miles per hour, it must have about 1/3 of a horsepower.

"I don't think your logic is right Mathew" stated

Ghanna. "Did you factor in the weight of the car? Or the fact that it has wheels? Was that an aerodynamically slippery car or a blocky SUV? What if it were going straight up instead of sideways?"

"Wow, you are right. It's getting very complicated. We do not have enough information to compute it." Trinny added.

"Hold on" said Bobba, excitedly waving his hand. "I found this information. The space shuttle needed about 15 million horsepower to overcome Earth's gravitational pull and get to the International Space Station."

Another kid chimed in. "If we approximate that

an astronaut in her spacesuit is 15 millions times lighter than the shuttle, then I estimate she would need a million consecutive farts to achieve escape velocity and propel herself into outer space."

"That's impossible. Even Grek couldn't fart that much even if he had a never-ending supply of refried beans to eat during the trip."

"There wouldn't be anyone left to watch after the farts gassed them out of the country," giggled another and everyone had a good chuckle. But still the kids went on and on using logic to prove or dispel their notions of fart powered spaceflight.

For the rest of the week, they kept up the debate and the research, but still they couldn't come to a definitive conclusion, so no one could be declared a winner, except for Bobba and his smelly stumper. But they all agreed that the laughs they had together and the knowledge they gained made them all winners.

Amongst the 5th graders, Math was no longer dull and mind-numbing. Now it offered them a way to indulge their divergent thinking and be liberated of the taboos adults placed on them. It was fun for the kids and educational enough to keep the adults from prying into the source of their chortles. And their game began to spread to other groups at Dozzaff. 99.99999% of the kids loved playing with Math this way. While some parents and teachers applauded their ingenuity, nonetheless their "dirty talk" was banned; school had no place for disgusting conversations. But they wouldn't be stopped. Did the ban actually make the games more desirable?! The kids thought so.

CHAPTER THREE
MORE YET TO SOLVE

O ver the next couple of weeks, Amby pulled himself away from the Math based amusement to focus on something more important. It was almost time to face off against the Scandaville Aces, the best soccer team around and the longtime rival of the Plaintown Zest soccer team that Amby captained. The Zest hadn't beaten the Aces in years, mostly because even in the 5th grade the kids of Scandaville were already 6' tall. It was a home game for Amby's team and he really wanted to beat them this year. He had poured through all of the Geometry and Physics books in the library to create some new plays that would help them win against their oversized opponents. The coach and his teammates had been very responsive; they had been running drills every day after school and on weekends to get ready for the confrontation.

A soccer game is very fluid, and the players need to be able to react both physically and mentally. Each time a player has possession of the ball, there are variety of possibilities to move forward. The possessor can dribble the ball forward to get past the defenders directly. Or they can pass to a teammate on the right, the left, or down field. They can kick the ball backward, then sprint towards the opponent's

goal to be ready to receive a long kick to start the attack.

No matter what the side with the ball is doing, the opposing players never stand idly by. Each player works their hardest to steal the ball and then move the game to the opposite side of the field. Simply put, there are 20 active players on the pitch fighting for control of the single soccer ball. As the player with the ball makes a choice, the other 19 players make their own choices based on what is happening and how the play could go based on their years of experience. The best teams have smart players who are talented on the pitch, but also in tune with their teammates so that they can work as a cohesive whole and not a gaggle of individuals. And they have to understand each opponent to make instinctual predictions about what they might do through each twist and turn of the game. To top that off, players must utilize their body mass in the most efficient way to position themselves in the right place to get the ball or disrupt the play while meting out their energy so they can last the whole game. Soccer is a mentally and physically intense sport.

Amby was already smart and strong on the field, and when he got that right trigger in Math class, it was like a new part of his brain suddenly came to life. He was already a smart cookie; he just needed a different way of looking at numbers to master Math.

Before we get back to the soccer showdown, let's take a short detour to see what kind of strategies Amby had cooked up using the fundamentals of math and science, and how they can be applied on the soccer pitch.

1. Pythagoream Theorem

Even though Amby was quick, able to sprint faster than many adults, he could never outrun a kicked soccer ball. So passing was the most efficient way to get the ball downfield so his team would have more opportunities to score.

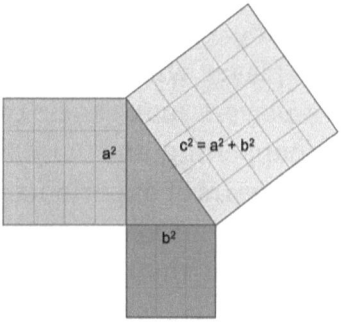

He knew passing the ball in triangle shapes was popular in soccer, but he wanted to understand why. Turns out it's because of the Pythagoream Theorem. When he and his teammates positioned themselves in the form of a right triangle, then kicking to the teammate on the diagonal (the hypotenuse of the triangle) was faster because it's a shorter distance than passing along the edges of the triangle (and through the

2nd player). An ideal choice when there weren't defenders getting in the way.

When passing along the hypotenuse is blocked, then of course he would have to pass along the sides of the right triangle in order for his team to keep possession (purple arrows in the diagram below). However, he could form a different triangle with another teammate behind him, and let his friend pass diagonally, or back to Amby, or to intercept another teammate in an unguarded position downfield (darker arrows below).

The decision Amby or any player made depended heavily on each situation; the weather, the condition of the pitch, their teammates' positions and skills, and the capability of each opposing players they are dealing with. All of these complicated decisions had to be made within a split second while the players are on the move. Quite the workout for the body and the mind to be a great player on a great team.

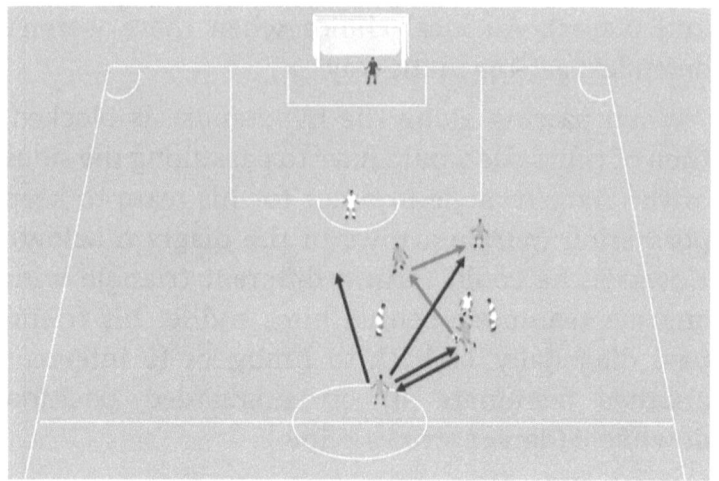

2. Projectiles in Motion

In sports, whenever a player makes a good shot, a lot of people write that off as luck instead of skill, after all it's easier to believe you lost to chance rather than being outplayed. Amby used to believe this too, but with his new interest in math and science, he felt compelled to dig deeper and understand the why of what happened. After a couple of "lucky" scores during practice, he spent some time doing research to explain the motion of the ball and went back out to better understand the physics and to perfect his technique.

A common notion is that to kick the ball really far all you have to do is kick it really hard, meaning there are only two variables in the equation: the kicker and the ball. To some extent, this is true based on Newton's Third Law of Motion; "for every action, there is an equal and opposite reaction." Therefore, to increase the action on the ball, or the force, to make it go further, Amby would have to do two things: 1) Increase the mass of his kicking leg, and 2) Improve his muscular strength to be able to accelerate his leg as quickly as possible. That was why Amby tried to eat well with the food his family could afford, to gain more mass, but he also worked hard on training his body to make sure he was adding muscle mass and increasing his speed to produce the best strength for his different kicks.

However, the universe is not that uncomplicated. After the ball is kicked, new forces come into play to change the ball's motion and to slow it down. The most impactful of them is gravity. While every object with mass has its own gravity, in our daily lives the only gravitational body that really affects us is the ground upon which we stand - Earth. The same force that helps us not float off into the void is also the one that complicates knowing just how far a ball will go. Amby knew that in the absence of understanding and skill, his success was not assured, no matter how physically strong and fast he could get. He needed to advance his knowledge of how gravity could affect his kicks.

To get the most distance, Amby knew he needed to get the ball off of the ground because the friction of the grass always robbed the ball of speed. Amby went to the pitch to run an experiment: what would happen when he varied how much loft he imparted to the ball on each kick while using the same force every time. First, he kicked the ball at a 15° angle, but the ball didn't go really far, only good for a short pass. Then he kicked the ball at a 45° angle and it traveled twice the distance, perfect for getting the ball downfield in a hurry! That was an amazing experiment, so he decided to take it up a notch and see if an even larger angle would launch the ball further. At a 75° angle, his ball went way high up, but didn't land much further away than his 1st shot at 15°, which wasn't really good unless his teammate was really good at headers and all that hang time would give the opponents too much time to try for a steal. Amby was frustrated that this was the opposite of what his prior kicks had showed. But he tried once again, pushing the limits to kick the ball straight up in the air at a 90° angle, only to have it land right next to him, almost conking his noggin; definitely not useful in a game.

He tested many more kicks of different angle but the results were consistent – kicks at 45° always gave the longest shots and any at a steeper or shallower angle came up short. Amby knew he had missed something and went home to check. Fortunately for him, the physics book had a whole chapter on the study of launching objects long distances, called Ballistics Theory. Gravity pulls down on all objects equally, regardless of their direction of travel. When he kicked the ball straight up, all his force was consumed to move it vertically and it got really high, but gravity was always pulling it straight downward, so it returned to its starting spot. But kicking the ball forward, with a low angle didn't get it very far because gravity exerted a large force on it and he hadn't given it enough upward motion to counteract gravity. In order to maximize the horizontal range of the ball, he needed to give the ball enough upward motion to offset gravity's pull the longest and enough forward motion to get it to go far. Evenly dividing the energy he gave the ball between upwards and forwards was why 45° was the perfect angle for his long distance kicks.

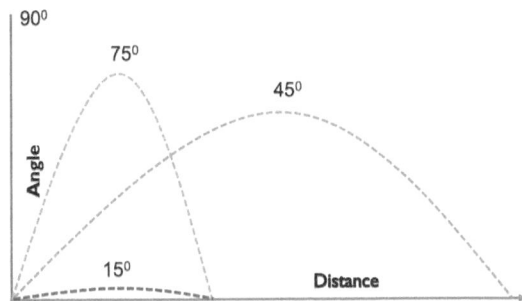

Now that he knew what he needed to do, Amby spent hours practicing his leg and foot positions so that he could unfailingly kick the ball at the perfect angle and speed for any situation. That's not so hard when standing still, but Amby had to practice while he was on the move, like in a real game. And he had to dodge around imaginary opponents, who were always trying to steal the ball for themselves. No matter how tired he felt, Amby's dream propelled him forward; he knew developing these skills were critical to achieving success.

3. The Coordinates

Running around in triangles and knowing how to boot the ball far are all great and well, but it wouldn't mean anything if the team didn't know where they needed to be on the field for each play. As Amby had mentioned in Math class, the pitch could be divided up into four pieces, or quadrants. So, Amby drew up diagrams to help the Coach and his team understand where on the field they needed to be based on where their opponents were. It took some time for everybody to get used to applying this new system, but it quickly became clear that it was worth the effort.

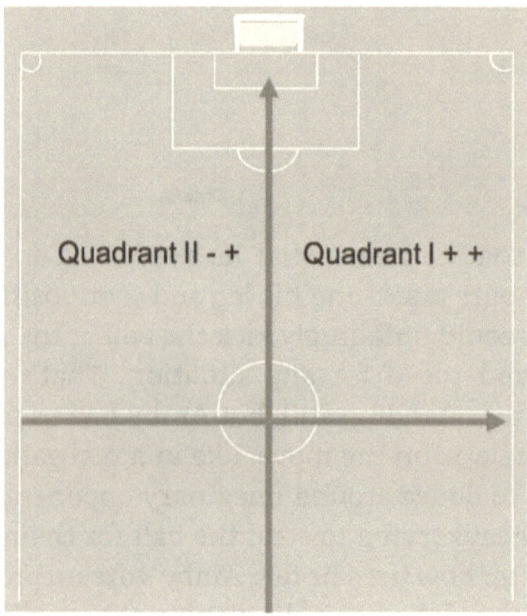

Since the Aces were always aggressive in attacking,

the quadrants made it easy for the Zest to know how to counter-attack. From past games, they learned that the Aces were so used to dominating the field, that even their defenders and goalie went to midfield and sometimes tried to score themselves. That meant the Zest's side would never be vacant of opponents. But having their foes' end field so empty would give Amby and the team a number of opportunities to use their new skills. The Aces tended to favor their right-side defenses (Quadrant II on Amby's diagram) so the Zest would utilize long passes with extreme diagonals down to Quadrant I and come at their opponent's goal from the weak side. Then, when the Aces all started to crowd Quadrant I, Amby's team would reverse the play by passing to and attacking from Quadrant II. Some kids didn't get it at first, but a couple of short scrimmages showed them how powerful the new system was.

The team's days were filled with practice to improve their physical skills and hone their foot angles and speed. To have a chance of besting the Aces, each Zest player would have to be a strong kicker, a fast runner and deadly accurate to put the ball exactly where their mates needed. The tools Amby showed them really helped the players boost their mental fortitude and maximize the value of their exertions. They all thanked Amby dearly for this new ways of thinking and playing.

When game day came, they were prepared and

confident. The Aces had skills and size, but the Zest knew it would only take one mistake by the Aces for them to capitalize and win the match.

The Aces had won the coin toss, so when the referee blew the starting whistle, their mid-forwarder gently passed the ball to the offense on the right. As usual, this over-confident player decided to show off by doing some rainbows while moving the ball down the field. A Zest mid-fielder dashed in from behind with his leg high up to attack the ball. Surprised by the move, the Aces' forwarder turned his back to keep the ball, sprinted up, and far-passed the ball down to the other offense. The sudden attack really disturbed his precision. The ball ended up right at the feet of a Zest defender, which he neatly trapped with his left foot, switched it to his right foot to avoid an Aces' forward, and then lofted the ball to his teammate on the right. Since the ball looked to be buried on the Zest's side, the rest of the Aces predictably poured downfield because they were certain that they would be able steal the ball back and go on the offense.

Seeing the incoming wave, the Zest defense continued passing the ball back and forth to each other, frustrating the Aces' forwards, and biding their time until the rest of the Aces got to midfield. Then, with a beautiful arcing kick, a Zest defender launched the ball along the right side far down into Quadrant I, just like they practiced. Allen, their mid-fielder, was right there to receive the ball. He signaled Amby to get in position, then chipped the ball for a perfect long pass. Facing his teammate, Amby lifted his leg to stop the ball with the top of his right foot, then pulled his foot back to land it on the ground in a split second. Aces were lumbering back to their side; they were big but not fast in this abrupt turnaround. There was only one defender in front of their penalty box. Amby turned toward the Aces' goal and swung his left leg backwards like he was going to make a powerful kick. The defender and the goalie both dashed to the side. But as Amby's left leg came in, it suddenly planted and Amby's right leg booted the ball into the completely open side of the goal, so fast that the opponents barely had time to blink in disbelief.

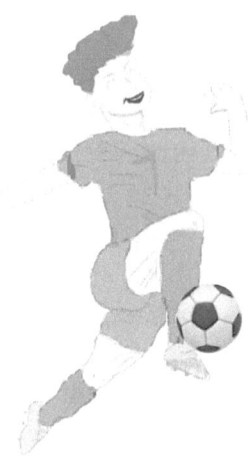

The sight of the grumpy Aces' goalie fishing the ball out from the net sure put a dent in that team's confidence. As the Zest ran back towards their side to reset, their supporters burst out into raucous cheers at the audacious and early score. They jumped up and down, whistled like crazy and made the bleachers boom as they did all kinds of funky dance moves in celebration. Even though Amby's folks were at work to support the family, his little sister was there to celebrate her brother's goal.

The referee blew his whistle to resume the game, pulling everybody back to reality. This time, the Aces passed the ball back to their half and tossed it around for a while. They purposefully slowed down the play to collect themselves. It looked like they were calculating something.

After a few minutes, the Aces started forwards, moving at a very deliberate pace. As they advanced, they spread out a bit but were running in packs of 2 or 3. This wasn't a strategy the Zest had seen before and now they were having to guess at their opponents' next moves, which meant they couldn't play as fast as before. However, their spirits were still high after Amby's incredible goal, so when the ball traveled to their half, they didn't hold back. Zippy, the left-swing forward, sped up and stuck his leg behind an Aces' midfielder to steal the ball. His opponent was very skillful and protected the ball as he rotated, then swiftly passed it to their midfield forward. Two more Zest players darted up to mark the Aces' mid-forward to stop him. But he was a very good player; he spun his body, crossed his feet to block the steal, and dashed downfield lickety-split. Zest supporters on the benches went quiet and crossed their fingers as the visiting team started playing instead of showing off.

Fortunately, the Zest defenders had practiced for

this situation. One on one, the Aces had more playing prowess, so when the Zest had to go on defense, they would utilize their smart strategies more than their technical skills. Scanning the positions of the incoming Aces, the Zest defenders all moved forward to create an off-side trap because they knew the Aces would pass the ball forward. They did it perfectly and there was a smattering of claps from the stands. But a nanosecond before the ref would see the offsides play, an Aces' player smashed into one of the Zest defenders and tumbled to the ground. The referee saw the fall, but it was clear that the defender was not at fault so he waived everybody to play on; no foul. However, the incident pulled his attention away from the offside situation. John, the Zest goalie, dove to the left to block the kick from the Aces' striker, but at almost point-blank range, the ball cannoned past him and into the net.

Instantly, the Zest Coach and the Plaintown supporters erupted to protest the blatant offside foul from the Aces. But there was only one referee on the pitch (it was just a 5th grade game after all), and his whistle acknowledged the score was final

After equalizing the score, the Aces played a new kind of game: exhausting the Zest players physically and mentally. Being more skillful, they had no trouble achieving their objective. They passed the ball around slowly, and when a Zest dashed in for the

attack, they would easily pass the ball away at the last second and manage to land a hit on Zest players. They taunted the home team with foul words and rude hand signs, all the while using their colossal bodies and distracting noise to make sure the referee remained clueless.

For their part, the Zest tried, but dirty play by the Aces just continued to wear them down. They couldn't imagine a stronger team would resort to this demeaning strategy and they began to feel powerless and hopeless.

Nearing the end of the first half, the Aces went on the offense and accelerated down field. The Zest could see the attack coming, but the ruthless abuse of the Aces had done its job and the Zest were running on fumes and struggling to mount a counter attack. Fortunately, Amby had some pretty thick skin, and he pulled back and took up a defensive position.

An Aces' midfielder, spotting the weakest players, took the ball down the left wing, with two of his compatriots in close formation. The rest of the team grouped up again, just like right before their last goal. As the Aces neared the Zest goal, one trio managed to land right in front of the ref to block his view of the defenders.

Roger, the Aces' left-wing star, was eyeing to lob the ball into the box from his position on the sideline, but two exhausted Zest defenders were blocking his shot. So, he made the cautious choice and lofted the ball towards his teammate on the right-wing edge of the goal box. The Zest fans went deathly quiet; certain that the unmarked Aces' player would make an easy score.

Zest players who had been struggling to get back to the goal stopped short to watch the inevitable heart-breaking scene. They had been working hard to get better over the last weeks, but clearly it wasn't enough to outperform the Aces. Even though the game wasn't yet half over, an air of despair settled over the field.

But there was one Zest player on the move. Amby was sprinting towards the right side to try and block the receiver. He was closing in when he had a sudden thought. What if he didn't wait for the ball to land? Could he intercept it and save his team?

They say that time stands still in decisive moments. And in this moment, Amby's deep learning of physics kicked in, like some survival instinct in this "life or death" second of the game. To Amby, it was like watching a video in super slow motion as he mapped out the path of the ball and plotted his intercept to break the Aces' attack, but to the rest of the crowd it was merely a twinkle. In the next moment, the whole crowd saw Amby suddenly pivot and jump into the air.

It was like some surreal set of paintings; Amby rising up and turning almost horizontal; serenely floating through the sky. The ball was whizzing through the air towards Amby, and clearly it was going to pass over him. The Aces started to snigger at what they thought was a kid going bonkers. The crowd continued to hold their breath, focused on this diorama playing out in front of them, bewildered as to how it would end, but surly it would dash their chance for a win against their archenemies.

And then...

Amby was bringing his right leg up, past vertical and going towards his head...

And then there was the beautiful "thump" you get when you strike the ball just perfectly.

As the ball sailed away towards the Aces' side, there was confusion in the stands and on the field. Some people were rubbing their eyes as if what they had just witnessed wasn't real. Some were standing awestruck at the phenomenal prowess Amby had just displayed. And everyone was trying to figure out how Amby had managed to get to the ball and execute, what they would later find out, an overhead kick, that only a few of the best professional soccer players could do. His teammates knew he was good, but this was beyond any skill he'd ever demonstrated in practice.Even before the fans were able to shake their hushed reverence, even before the thuds of the ball bouncing hard on the pitch registered with the home team, the Aces were already on the attack. While the Zest were still lost in their star player's act of grandeur, an Aces' striker swiftly received the ball and the visiting team rapidly formed up for their strike. An Aces' winger dashed into the box to lure the Zest goalie toward him. Blocking the goalie's movement, he passed the ball out for his teammate to finish.

Down by one, the Zest plodded to the side to huddle up as the halftime whistle sounded.

The Zest sideline was a state of pandemonium. Some players were aggressively vocal about finding ways to expose how the Aces had been cheating to manipulate the game. Some players were moaning that their skills weren't up to snuff and they didn't know how to get better by the start of the next half. But they all agreed that their sense of fair play mandated that everybody should have a nondiscriminatory chance to excel in the actual sport and the underhanded tactics of the Aces had to be stopped. But how could they dispel their opponents' mischievousness?

One clear option was to make sure the referee could actually see the field by breaking up Aces' "filthy task-force". But there were risks, so the team hastily made a verbal list of pros and cons.

On the positive side:

• Annulling the Aces' unsportsmanlike conduct and putting them on notice that the Zest knew what they were up to should discourage additional misbehavior.

• Playing a fair game and ensuring that the best team won.

• Maybe getting the Aces back on the straight and narrow.

But, on the other hand:

• The Aces could just get mad and be even more malicious in game, maybe even physically hurting the Zest players.

- Spending more time watching the other players and trying to police the game rather than playing it.
- Knowing that even if they won, it would be a hollow victory because it wouldn't be 100% based on their skill.

Another option was to not focus on fair, but stoop to Aces' level and play just as dirty as they did.

The benefits of this tactic would be:

- Wouldn't lose any players to watch the opposition – they would all be in the game and fighting to win.
- Showing that they weren't a team to be trifled with.
- Teaching the Aces that what goes around comes around.

However, on the negative side:

- They would have to debase themselves by not playing a clean game.
- Letting down their families and friends who would see them being foul on the field.
- Knowing that even if they won, it would be a hollow victory because it wouldn't be 100% based on their skill.

As they debated these options amongst themselves, a warry eye on the clock counting towards the start of the second half, it was clear that they were stuck in "a damned if you do, damned if you don't conundrum." None of the Zest players were there for a fight; they just wanted to play a soccer game with everyone trying their best, playing fair and square, and knowing the winner was truly the best team on the pitch that day. They loved the work of improving their skills, enjoyed the artistry and physics of a well-placed shot, the physical demands of chasing down and intercepting the ball, the trill of a perfectly executed play as a team, pushing the limits of their minds and bodies to make themselves better on and off the pitch.

Soccer, like any other sport, is supposed to be a game, not an end in and of itself. It's about fun, camaraderie and growth; about discipline, honor, and perseverance. From the players just starting out to the paradigms of the sport, the rules are there to create a level playing field. Players show up for each game because of the joy of competition, not because of some perverse idea of fun that involves hurting other players on purpose.

Every kid on the Zest aspired to be like one of the greats, to have such high technical skills that they seemed to be acrobats and magicians rolled into one. They had watched reruns of games with Pele and Maradona, who moved so fast they looked like streamers of silk that blurred across the TV screen, soccer ball at their feet like it was magnetically attached, cutting through the defenders like they were standing still. Or Messi playing keep away with his team, like they knew what the defenders were thinking, and then suddenly popping the ball into the bottom of the net before anyone had even realized he had taken the shot. Or Beckham seemingly breaking the laws of physics by making some fantastic kick to send the ball on an impossible trajectory, just millimeters inside the goal and out of reach of the keeper.

Now, suppose these world-class players had chosen to use their skills to cheat? If the best devolved, everyone else would have to follow just to try and keep up, and the sport would just become an empty shell that players and fans alike would turn away from. The popularity of soccer, the way it transcends nations and class, is because it is accessible to all and it is a game of true skill and teamwork, not a modern-day version of a gladiatorial pit. With merely a roundish ball and some empty space to practice and play, anyone could rise to the top if they invested enough time, energy, and brain power to create their own miracles. Soccer presents opportunities for everybody, equally.

Thus, if any of the Zest wanted to be in the pantheon of soccer legends one day, they had to play by the rules. They would follow in the footsteps of the greats by working hard, cultivating their teamwork and advancing their abilities so that no dirty players could knock them down.

In short, they would keep calm and carry on NICELY and FAIRLY.

Winning was important, but mastering their basic instincts in tough situations, maintaining their morality, was their path to everlasting fulfillment. That would be their ultimate victory.

The team had their strategy for the second half.

The Zest had the kickoff for the second half and they started off defensively, keeping possession of the ball while seeing what the other team was up to. Amby and the Coach could see that the Aces hadn't given up on their disreputable tactics, and they used hand signals to keep the rest of their team focused on the game and not on the Aces' tricks.

As the Zest made a move to drive downfield, a couple of the Aces sped up, used some distractions, and stole the ball away. Reverting to form, the Aces started to toy with the host team, doing rainbows and sombreros to get the Zest mad and off balance. The Zest tried their best to get the ball back, but just like a game against the Harlem Globetrotters, it's hard to play when your foes were bending the rules and doing stunts.

Roger got the ball and started a dash towards the Zest goal and two more Aces got into position inside the box. The referee moved down to watch the play, with three Aces hot on his heels, to be "in position" when the play came. Amby signaled his goalkeeper and defenders to be ready as two more Aces raced into the box. Roger turned toward the goalie but lobbed the ball across to a teammate. One defender jumped up to trap the ball with his chest, but as he came down, he fell on an Aces' player who wasn't there a second ago. The Scandaville player rolled onto his side, mewling like a little kitten as his comrade was already reporting the foul to the ref.

None of the Zest was really sure what had happened because their attention was focused elsewhere. It seemed likely that the Aces' player had purposely slotted in to take the hit, but maybe it was just an accident. All the referee could do was to use his straightforward reasoning: there was no protest coming from the Zest and the Aces were aggressive about the penalty, so that's the way he called it.

As the Aces lined up for the penalty kick, the Zest were sure they were about to lose another point after losing two in the first half. Their goalie looked tense, pacing to the left and the right like a caged animal, alternating his gaze between the ground and the sky. As the referee blew his whistle, a calm came over the goalkeeper as he steeled himself for the Aces' assault.

The Aces' best striker walked to the right, paused for a moment and then zoomed towards the ball. He turned his right foot to 45° for a powerful kick; however, he swiftly extended the angle to over 100° right before executing his confident launch. A very skillful shoot indeed!

But there was NO swoosh of the ball hitting the net.

Arrayed on the side for the penalty shot, Amby watched the scene closely. When the ball ended up in the hands of the goalie, neither was surprised as they slyly shared a broad smile.

The rest of the field was deathly quiet. Everyone was so stunned and discombobulated at what had just happened, that there was no cheering at the amazing save.

As mentioned earlier, soccer is no simple game. The constantly unpredictable movement of the ball among the twoscore players means only the sharpest could survive and thrive in soccer. You have to be smart and strong to be among the best players. The players need keen senses to absorb data on the game around them: they have to track the ball, watch where their teammates and opponents are, and deduce where they'd go next; pay attention to the wind speed and direction as well as the turf conditions to know how every kick and pass would be affected; and like a giant chess game, try and stay several moves ahead to achieve the optimal outcome. But unlike chess, where the players could take as long as they wish to make their next move, in soccer decisions have to be made instantly, while the players are still in motion. Although it seems super human, it's really a matter of basic science. Neuroscientists have shown that our brains are neuroplastic; meaning we can teach ourselves to accomplish almost anything so long as we spend enough time training. When we start learning a new skill, our brains mainly use working memory to process information and develop new neural pathways, which causes learning to be slow. With repeated training, the neurons that are wired together will fire together, and we start using our long-term memory to be able to act faster without having to resort to the working memory. This is often referred to as instinct, intuition, muscle memory – where we seem to act and react without any real thought. It's not true that there's no thinking involved; we're still making logical choices, but our repeated experience and practice make it look effortless. Every person, regardless of biological inheritance or socioeconomic standing is capable of this, as long as they put in the work.

But enough discussion about the intricacies of neuroscience for now. Let's focus on that fantastic save.

John, the Zest's keeper, hadn't been nervous, he was actually studying his surroundings to anticipate how the ball might change in flight. And he and Amby shared a little telepathy to remind John to breathe and focus. So, when John saw the striker go for the kick, he watched the kicker's feet to know which way to dive to get in front of the ball. Although he saw his opponent's right foot change angle just before it came into contact with the ball, he was also focused on his left foot as it planted for the kick. He and Amby had spent a lot of time practicing and John knew that the angle of the non-kicking foot, which the kicker used to balance himself, gave a clear indication of which direction the ball would go. And once the kicking leg was in motion, it couldn't change so much to be independent from the non-kicking leg without upsetting the player's balance; thus it was the non-kicking foot that telegraphed how high or low and into what corner of the net the ball would go. While it looked like magic to so many, it was really John expressing his finely honed talents.

With a quick wink to his teammates and empowered by the stupendous block, John punted the ball all the way downfield, in a perfect parabolic arc, straight towards the opposing goal. While the Aces stood paralyzed watching the ball sail downfield, Amby and the rest of the team darted away at full speed to get the ball and drive towards the goal. Frightened into action, an Aces' defender clumsily crashed into the boy to break the attack. Unfortunately for the defender, the other Aces near the referee were still rooted in place and the ref had a clear line of sight to the blatant foul. A free kick for the Zest was on the menu.

The Zest supporters came alive. Not that Amby had taken a hit, but because they had finally recovered from the earlier shock and were making up for lost time. Their spirits had been low at the end of the first half, but with that last play, they were thinking that their team could really pull off a win today. Amby's little sister waved a large flag while shouting his name in encouragement. The home team fans clapped hands, stomped their feet and chanted: Zest – Zest – Zest!!!

Most of the Aces retreated to build their defensive line in front of the goal, with a couple of strikers left on the Zest side to be ready for a fast counter-attack if Amby's kick was blocked.

Amby placed the ball down where the ref had marked, scanned his surrounding and closed his eyes in thought. 25 minutes was left on the clock, more than enough time for the Aces to score again. He needed to seize this opportunity to score to help his team get excited and put the Aces off balance.

He was 20 yards away from their goal, the wind was blowing into his face, and he was staring at a colossal wall of bodies. The giant Aces were so wide and tall that they blocked any direct shot. Amby signaled some peers to get into position so they could receive his pass and shoot around the defenders. Then he walked back a few feet to get a running start at the kick.

With the Aces' defenders eyeing the Zest strikers moving in, they missed the kick and only refocused to find the ball lobbed up high at an angle that was sure to take it over the left corner of their goal. A couple of their defenders had the presence of mind to jump up for a block just in case, but to avoid getting smashed in the face, they tucked their chins into the necks to use their foreheads to repel the ball.

After having analyzed all information, Amby knew there was only a small gap between the human blockade and the goalie's reach at the very top corner of the goal. He would have to lift the ball up and make it change direction in flight to slot it into the net. His study of physics and his avid soccer watching told him his only chance was to bend it like Beckham.

Usually for a strong kick and good lift, a player kicks the ball straight on and at the bottom. To "bend the ball", Amby would have to use the Magnus force to impart some spin to the ball while kicking it. To achieve this, Amby placed the instep of his kicking foot slightly up from the bottom and slightly to the outside of the ball for power and loft. Then, as he was following through on the kick, he pulled his leg across his body to impart the necessary spin. As the ball moved through the air, the pressure around it was unequal: the outside, where it had been kicked, experienced a higher pressure than the inside. Just like an airplane wing that is drawn upwards by the low pressure above it, so too was the ball sucked inwards. As the ball lost momentum from the kick, the Magnus force had a stronger impact and the ball abruptly swerved away from its path of travel and dropped down just below the top bar of the goal and on the opposite side of where the goalie expected. His love of the game and dedication had really paid off for Amby. He closed his eyes and smiled broadly on the inside. Science was pure magic.

The crowd blinked. They were stunned having witnessed something they had only ever seen on TV, and from this young kid. While their brains debated what they had just seen, the ref's whistle to acknowledge the goal shook them out of their contemplation and a hurricane of sound enveloped the field. Even some of the Aces' fans cheered in awe of the talent displayed.

The Zest confidently and cheerfully moved back to their side. The Aces kicked the grass and mumbled as they assembled at half field to resume the game. There was an evil glint in their eyes; the Zest could see that this 2-2 tie wouldn't stand for long.

The referee whistled for the game to continue.

The Aces ramped up their aggressiveness as they kicked off. The center striker passed the ball to Roger, who sent head signals to different Aces across the field. As he passed the ball to the right side, a Zest mid-fielder jumped up to intercept it with his chest. Up in the air, the Zest player suddenly found himself trapped between two incoming Aces. He tried to tilt to the right to avoid the leg of the player on his left, but that put him into the lofty knee from the other opponent. He took a direct hit to his chest and tumbled to the ground. In pain, he staggered to his feet to keep playing.

The referee waived his arms. No foul. The game resumed.

Pizz, one of the Aces' strikers, had the ball and made a long pass back towards the middle of the field, right towards a couple of Zest players. As the Zest tried to gain control of the ball, a group of Aces crashed into them making a hostile play for the ball. No foul again. The Zest knew the Aces could dole out this punishment for the rest of the game without breaking a sweat, and it was only a matter of time before they would be too incapacitated to put up a defense.Time and again, the Aces put the ball where they could make contact with a Zest player while making it look like it was just a fair battle for control of the ball. The Aces' cheating was so smooth, it was hard for anyone but the players on the field to see they were playing dirty. The host team was losing steam again and started to fear an inevitable, humiliating defeat by their archenemy.

Amby and the whole team heard the same shout in their heads 'This needs to stop.' The team had vowed to play the game to the highest standard, so they were puzzled how could they stop this war of attrition being inflicted upon them.

Another "pass" was inbound from the Aces, and

headed straight towards Amby, along with multiple enemy combatants. Seeing that he could not avoid getting crushed in an Ace sandwich, Amby harnessed all the strength he had built up in his years of intensive training and the mental urge to nullify his unscrupulous opponents. He leapt straight up into the air a good ten feet and watched as the Aces ended up slamming into each other after his sudden departure. As he sprang up, the ball came with him, and he used hand signals to communicate a change of strategy to his teammates. At first, his friends looked up as if to say "Are you kidding me?" and shook their heads. However, once they tried to lift up their bodies, they flew up like a feather in an updraft. It felt weird for a second, standing around in midair, then they embraced the new reality that the Aces could no longer interfere with them. The team started to pass the ball around and take control of this new soccer pitch above the reach of their monstrous opponents. This was super-duper cool!

On the ground, the Aces and the all of the fans were rubbing their eyes, desperate to dispel what must surely be a mass hallucination. Then the Aces started running and jumping, trying to get into the air themselves or at least manage to yank one of the Zest to the ground, but to no avail. The home team was playing on a whole different level. Literally.

In a couple of minutes, Amby and his team got some much-needed relief away from the bruisers down below and mastered how to rapidly elevate to the floating pitch and descend smoothly to the ground. For while they were up high, the goals were still on the ground, so any attack would necessitate running three dimensional plays.

Up in the air, they could talk without being overheard by the visitors, so Amby hurriedly formulated some new plays to confound the ground bound clods and win this game.

Midair, with the ball still in their possession and the referee too stunned to even try and call a delay of game penalty, the Zest kicked the ball back and forth a few rounds to draw the Aces' attention. Then someone suddenly sent a long pass down to Amby, who was running on the ground just shy of the Aces' goal box. As the ball neared him, he stopped and made a U-turn to face the ball as if he was going to pass the ball back to their side. Instead, he jumped and laid back, brought his right leg up, and delivered a fatal bicycle kick. 3-2 Zest.

Even with five minutes left, the crowds poured onto the pitch like the game was over. The referee, the Coach, and the Zest players had to herd the throng back to sidelines to finish.

At the kickoff, the Zest had to be on the ground lest they give the Aces a wide-open shot on goal. But the Aces had no more self-control left, so the kickoff was more like a bazooka fired at the enemy. The first Zest player took the hit straight in the abdomen and flew backwards a couple of feet. The Aces were like savage animals, clawing and hissing at their opponents as they went after the ball, kicking it towards any unfortunate Zest player at hand. As one Zest player reached down to help up his teammate, they suddenly realized that they were the targets. Huddling together, they witnessed the incoming projectile suddenly divert away from them, as if it had bounced off of something, like a shield. Another Zest ran up to them and instantaneously they could feel an energy field around them, protecting them. So as the Aces continued their rampage, the Zest fell back towards their goal, collecting their team as they went, and feeling their protective bubble grow. They might not be able to stop the Aces' insanity, but they could make sure that this force would protect their goal until the time ran out.

As the Zest reached their end of the field and connected with John in goal, Pizz was only five feet away when he delivered a kick so hard that the soccer ball seemed to go oblong as it sped towards the center of the Zest's mass. Instead of bouncing off, the ball touched the shield and hovered in the air, spinning around as if calculating what to do next.

Unexpectedly, the ball flashed back to Pizz and hit him in the head and rebounded off of him to smash into the shoulder of his teammate. Like some possessed snooker ball, it continued around, using the Aces like billiards bumpers, hitting heads, knees, stomachs, knocking them one and all to the ground. With Roger the only one of the Aces still standing, the ball hit him in the posterior as he had turned to run away. With the impact, there was something like a sonic boom and a ghastly smell tainted the air.

With all of the Aces prostrated across the field, faces skyward, the ball went zooming into the heavens. Then like a hawk finding its prey, it crashed hard into the tummy of a supine player. The resulting borborygmus was almost painfully loud, but before anyone could shield their ears, a fountain of vomit erupted from the boy's mouth. The ball proceeded to hit the stomachs of the other players, eliciting a rumble and a stream of puke from each. Around and around the ball went, in a rhythmic pattern, a torrent of gas and upchuck in its wake. The sunset reflected on the shooting liquid made the scene truly second to none. Some would later say that the torrents of sick and flatulence were on par with the best water fountain shows they had ever seen.

At the beginning, all were bemused at the way the Aces were being castigated by a soccer ball. But as the discipline escalated, the crowed fell silent. Just as they were starting to feel both sorry for the Aces and awed at the fanciful fluids, the referee tweeted his whistle to signal the end of the game. And the ball dropped to the ground, an inert sphere once again.

As the Aces crawled to their bus in abject humiliation, the crowd came to their feet to cheer on the Zest. To their credit, the Zest tried to help their foes to their feet, but the Aces refused all help; even now, too stubborn to admit defeat.

So as the sun descended on Plaintown, the town headed home to enjoy a well-deserved respite from the day's tribulations.

But there was one resident who did not head home. Passed out on the hill overlooking the soccer field, was Mr. Troubar.

While Amby and the rest of the school had gone about their business as usual, Mr. Troubar had stayed fixated on ascertaining the changes that had come over the kids. He had been watching them surreptitiously in school and today he was up on the hill away from the crowd, using his tools to watch the game from afar, looking for any sign or signal. He had spent his evenings setting up his spy cameras all round the field, to make sure he missed no details. Up on the hill he had his screens to watch and record what the cameras saw, plus some old school tech of a telescope and a pair of binoculars.

From his string of spent nights, he knew his goal wasn't going to be easy to attain. Peering through the various lenses, staring at his laptop and scrubbing through the various angles and coverage for the whole game wasn't easy and took a toll on his body. His arms ached, his legs wanted to fall off, his eyes burned, his back hurt, and his gut rumbled in hunger. Worse still, for all his time and effort, there was no scintilla of proof on how Amby and the team were doing these amazing things, and that bothered him dearly. His detective mission wasn't satisfactory in any sense.

As he sulked beneath the tree, his brain was a ball of contradictions, each fighting for dominance of his thoughts. On the one hand, he was certain Amby had been using some skullduggery to get ahead in class. In all his years of teaching, not even his most gifted students had ever attained that level of academic competency overnight. And yet, the boy had showed consistent mastery of the subject ever since that fateful day. A cheater would eventually screw up and reveal their disgrace, but Amby was unflappable. He despaired of ever substantiating his hunches.

Intuitively, Mr. Troubar was convinced that Amby's pauses before answering were designed to give him time to summon some kind of help. Although the help was not overtly evident, it had to exist in some form. Logically, he reasoned that pausing was a natural human reaction as their synapses fired, linking neurons together in deep contemplation of the tricky subject matter. Maybe he had seen the Math problems, or something similar, and Amby's brain had been searching for the solution. However, a game of soccer didn't have a predefined answer; it wasn't a static problem on the page to be solved, it was a perpetually dynamic equation that could only be parsed as it occurred. Nevertheless, Amby was like some modern-day Merlin, waving his hands about, turning around the game through force of will and wizardry.

Above all, he wasn't going to give up the assertion that he was the Doyen of Math. With all his training and hands-on experience, he was, without question, this generation's Gauss. But maybe, just maybe, his ego was blinding him to some unseen facet of human evolution. Was he witnessing progress that no scientist had even envisaged; some step function change in genetics? That might explain why his kids, with a gene that older generations didn't have, could improve their math skills so precipitously or respond instantaneously to the fluidity of the soccer.

With all of that swirling around in his brain, Mr. Troubar also had to contend with the ending of the game. Surely the inanimate ball hadn't evolved to emit antigravitons or develop a wicked sense of humor to humiliate the Aces. And even if it did, why didn't it go after the visiting team and the Zest equally? Was there a home team supporter in control of the ball, mystically saving the local boys and giving the intruders their comeuppance? No, it couldn't be true. As a strictly logical Math teacher, incantations had no place to exist in his mind. Period.

The disorder on the field that discombobulated the players and the crowd was nothing compared with the turmoil inside Mr. Troubar's head. Instead of finding answers, he had even more queries and problems to sort out. His brain was simply not up to the task and as it short circuited, he collapsed where he sat. Fortunately, he woke up at dawn and slunk home before any of the townsfolk could see him.

The next day, the whole town gathered to bask in the glory of the Zest's triumph. Tired and still puzzled, Mr. Troubar put his conflicted feelings aside to acknowledge the splendid achievement of the whole soccer team.

Many more mysteries await the Math teacher and the kids to solve. But for today, let us take this time to chronicle the Dozzaff School's milestone achievement!!!

EPILOGUE

What you have read so far is only the beginning of a fantastic journey as the parties try to unwind a mystery, and do a lot of learning about math, science and themselves.

We, the author, consider you, the readers, as participants in our story. Come join us and share your ideas on what might happen next. We promise to read all legible and politely worded submissions and incorporate the best ideas sent to stemdation@gmail.com.[‡]

[‡] Legal says we have to mention that all submissions become the property of the people behind Elec Twisiti. Credit will be afforded for ideas used, but there is no monetary compensation available. Okay – Legal says we might be able to provide a free copy of the aforementioned book where said ideas were credited – if we can wrest the book out of Legal's hands – and you know that's like trying to get a cookie away from a certain fuzzy blue guy.